DATE DUE

OCT 10 '85	JUN 20 '86	NO 6 '93	
NOV 2 '85	JUL 7 '86	DE 13 '93	
NOV 11 '85	JUN 9 '87	MR 2 '94	
DEC 3 '85	JUN 29 '87	JE 12 '94	
JAN 2 '86	JUL 23 '87		
JAN 30 '86	MAY 20 '88		
FEB 13 '86	JUN 25 '88		
FEB 28 '86	AUG 6 '88		
APR 4 '86	AP 7 '90		
APR 12 '86	FE 12 '93		
MAY 13 '86	FE 25 '93		
JUN 6 '86	MR 22 '93		

A Death in Irish Town

By the same author:

The Poor Old Lady's Dead
The Shallow Grave
A Clutch of Vipers
The Gospel Lamb
The Bastard's Name was Bristow
An Uprush of Mayhem
The Local Lads
Corporal Smithers, Deceased
All the Pretty People
A Time of Fine Weather

A Death in Irish Town

JACK S. SCOTT

St. Martin's Press
New York

Library of Congress Cataloging in Publication Data

Scott, Jack S.
A death in Irish Town.

"A Joan Kahn book."
I. Title.
PR6069.C589D4 1985 823'.914 85-11818
ISBN 0-312-18870-6

First Edition

10 9 8 7 6 5 4 3 2 1

A Death in Irish Town

1

Nostalgia, it was, that took Detective Inspector Alfred Stanley Rosher down to that unsalubrious part of the town where blank-eyed and blackened warehouses, abandoned now almost entirely, stand gazing glumly at the glum waters of the canal. In his heyday, nobody ever called him a sensitive man, given to pining wistfully backward; but of late, with retirement grinning frightfully into his face and old age gibbering ahead, he had been thinking more and more of the old days and the young copper that was. It happens, alas, to every man nearing the end of his useful life.

It was his first beat, this area known in those days as Irish Town. Peaceful enough now, with most of the slummy little streets bulldozed away and resurrected into council estates with cars standing at curbs outside nearly all the little houses. But he walked it first with a tough and seasoned veteran dead this many years, and later with a young Constable Dancey, now Sergeant Barney Dancey and soon to retire himself, because at that time policemen did not patrol down here singly. They ventured in pairs, especially when the pubs turned out.

It was a fire that brought him down. One of the old, tinder-dry warehouses, used for storing wool in the days when much of the town traffic was by barge and lighter along the canal. The oil contained in untreated fleeces, permeated for a hundred-odd years into dry timber floorings, adds wondrously to the timber's combustibility. The place went up with a whoosh, late on a calm September evening.

Detective Inspector Rosher heard about it just after he cleaned his big beige teeth and turned to his cluttered kitchen, seeking a usable frying pan in which to sizzle a wad of bacon and two eggs, to fortify himself against the day. His portable radio stood where he always put it, on the kitchen table beside the ketchup bottle, tuned to a merry early chat show which never claimed his ear—it pushed back the silence, that's all—except when a more urbane tone took over from the hysterically happy presenter to give the news bulletin.

Fried bread was growing crispy on its second side when the fire was mentioned. Firemen from the town augmented by the city brigade, the dulcet voice said, had kept it from spreading to buildings nearby. Nobody dead—nobody so much as injured. But for the flames leaping three hundred feet into the air, from the news point of view hardly worth bothering about, really, except for the local press and the city radio station.

The canal front flashed clearly onto the screen of Rosher's mind. Not surprising, he thought, as the frenzied hysteric took over to send a diamond wedding greeting to a Mr. and Mrs. Simmons of Wacket, Herts, who probably wheezed and chumbled and died from excitement over their milk-sopped Brekky-Wheat. Always said those bloody places were firetraps. Wonder they haven't all gone up long ago. And he sat himself down to eat his bacon, his eggs, and his fried bread, and to wash them down with black and bitter tea, two fillings of his pint mug, before he took himself off to court; where he spoke charitable words on behalf of one of his regulars, who drew six months in spite of it. The man gazed reproachfully at Rosher as he went down, having traded information for the favor of those words, which the inspector had said would get him off.

A lot of waiting around is done by policemen on days when they appear in court. Arriving punctually at ten, when the fun-filled day began, he sat in the annex among the little bent and their escorts, keeping himself as always to himself until the case was called at eleven-thirty. An hour and a half, with a bumble-talk going on now and again between other waiting policemen, touching often upon the fire. Still burning, they said.

It focused his idle mind: upon the old days, the good days, the days before marriage; the boxing days, the days of wine and roses. The days of the O'Haras—oh, the bloody O'Haras—the Kellys, and the O'Flaherties, rumbustious buggers all. Many of the families still living around there, but tamed now into the council houses, runners out into the country on blameless weekends in their little tin cars.

By twelve o'clock he was standing sunlit upon the steps of the handsome eighteenth-century courthouse, fixing the black Anthony Eden hat low upon the brow. Paperwork only awaited him at the station until this evening, when he expected to stand well back into the shadow of a doorway giving good view of a store specializing in hi-fi systems, casette recorders, and color TVs; from whence he would emerge, if the tip-off had a cast-iron bottom, to embrace two old friends in the act of manipulating a jimmy. Old-fashioned boys, they were. Your up-and-comer has better tools.

He hated paperwork. Who among CID men does not? Bugger it, he thought, it's lunchtime anyway, and his mind wandered again to the relatively paper-free and happy days of his sappy youth. The bus just drawing in over there, he said to himself, goes right past the canal basin. Sod it—they can spare me for an hour. If they haven't closed the Ring o' Roses because of the fire, it must be close by. I can get a pie and a pint.

Ten minutes later he was walking down from the main road, through the area of council estates already halfway back to the slumdom from which the planners—not realizing that slum-dwellers in general like to keep coal in the bath—had tried to deliver them when they cleared away the old mean streets.

It was not his first time back since he moved on, to a new beat and later into the CID. Once or twice he had visited, but briefly by car, and only to effect an arrest. Somehow, whatever villainy took place down here seemed to pass him by. Wherefore he looked around with interest now as he made for where black smoke still rose into the blue air, the destroyed warehouse itself hidden from him as yet. It was difficult to work out where they ran, Hay Street and Gomms Alley and Troop Street and all those evil little courts. They'd all gone, replaced by Coronation Avenue and Edinburgh

Crescent, Prince of Wales Terrace and the like, laid out on a grid. And nobody about whom he recognized.

But then, there wouldn't be. It was all of thirty years since this beat was his, and most of his iron-fisted, clog-booted tearaways would be senile by now. Or dead.

Two uniform constables stood by the same old bridge at the slope leading down to the canal basin. Recognizing him—and who, having seen him once, would fail to recognize the durable and apelike body swinging along in the durable blue serge suit, black hat low upon a remarkably simian brow?—they nodded as he passed through, boxy-toed shoes bearing him over cobbles onto the cobbled quay where the lighters and barges used to be loaded.

This, he knew, was a conservation area now, each of the grimed warehouses listed to hold the bulldozers at bay. One had gone before the order was clapped on to save the rest; the one this side of the fire. In its place had arisen a glass-and-concrete structure attached to a walled garage-and-courtyard area housing the trucks belonging to the haulage firm owned by an ex-mayor. There'd been a row about that, he remembered, out of which came the conservation order.

Surprizingly, no rubbernecks were here. The policemen at the bridge would have turned them away, of course, as they arrived, but normally they linger. Here were only firemen, and a tangle of hoses snaking to the three fire appliances left of the dozen that had worked, the radio had said, through the night. Obviously the fire was not completely extinguished. A man on a high ladder still directed his thick stream of chemical-augmented water down through a gap where part of the wall had collapsed, and other men operated hoses from ground level, squirting through the hole where the door had been. Smoke and steam still billowed upward. A superior fireman stood helmeted and alone, watching his men.

Rosher knew him. The firemen, the policemen, the ambulance teams in any town get to know each other. He walked across and said: "'Morning, Mr. Faith."

"Good morning, Mr. Rosher," the fire officer said. Very polite. They did not know each other all that well.

"Got yourself a big one."

"Wonder it's not bigger. I've been at 'em for years about it, public hazard some of these old places. I'd have 'em all down tomorrow. Lucky we got here before the lot went up."

"I thought some of 'em were being used?"

"Only that one, so far." The fireman pointed to the building next to the flamer. "There's all these plans, but up to now only the artie-crafties have moved in. Me, I'd have 'em out again."

"How do they stand, then, with the fire regulations?"

"They conform. Just about. Minimum standards. Wouldn't have helped 'em much, would it, if the whole bloody issue had gone? Tinder, that's what this lot is. Tinder. No other word for it."

"They'll all have to come into line, though, won't they, if they're filling 'em up?" That was the plan: the obsolete buildings, the whole basin, to be turned into an inland marina. The hire firm's narrowboats lay already at the quay lower down, gay with springtime painted traditional rose-and-castle decoration. A few privately owned cruisers occupied the first of the planned public moorings. There were day-boats for hire already, pay the hire-firm man; who was not here at the moment, but usually stood about in a yachting cap.

"Fat lot of good that'll do 'em. Small lets, aren't they? The souvenir shop's only got a ground floor and the basement. Miracle they didn't lose the lot, right next door like that. They'll all be surrounded by imminent death, soon as they move in." He spoke with gloomy relish, pleased with the phrase.

They wouldn't be. No living-in allowed, so they'd all go home in the evening. You need to be a veritable twannie not to notice, between the hours of nine o'clock and five-thirty, that the whole bloody place was crackling and luridly roaring all around you. But a dedicated man on a hobbyhorse has a right to a jolly good ride.

"Uh-huh," said Inspector Rosher. "Uh-hnn." He nodded the black hat, sagaciously.

The fire officer was a man no more given to small chat than was Rosher himself. They stood a while in silence, the inspector looking about him.

Not much had changed down here, considering the flying years.

The haulage firm's glass-glittering building was not here then, of course, and the grimy old workboats manipulated and lived in by families as prone to punch-up as the resident Irish—they used to use the Ring o' Roses, just along there—lay where the pretty cruisers were now. Some of the latter, closest to the fire, looked a bit scorched. Further down, the Happy Wanderer narrowboats had escaped unblistered. The water looked cleaner than it was.

The Ring o' Roses. The old Ring o' Roses. Bloody hell, there'd been some action there in the old days. How often did the mighty right fist of young P. C. Rosher, the awesome Hammer that made him Police All-England heavyweight champion for three years running, thunk home to subdue a Flanagan, an O'Flaherty, an O'Hara. Oh, the bloody O'Haras!

The Ring o' Roses. Happy days.

That hadn't changed much either, on the outside. They'd probably tarted the inside. Or perhaps they hadn't, because until the marina scheme was mooted, everything down here was abandoned, more or less. And the marina work started very recently and quite suddenly on a wave of conservationist–cum–tourist board enthusiasm sprung by the ex-mayor's demolition, for opening fully next spring.

If things were as they once were, you could get a pie and a pint there. Good bread and solid cheese, too, with a bloody great pickled onion, cost about fourpence. Too much to hope for such cheese now, they don't make it any more, nor the bread with the mighty crust. Nor do they bottle such onions. Those who did, and those who served them out from behind the bar—tough old Ted Oatie and his even tougher old lady—they'd all be gone by now. Probably dead. By heck, that made you think.

He grunted to the fire chief, who grunted back. It served as farewell. The black hat, the durable suit, the box-toed shoes turned. The whole man moved away on bandy legs too short, really, for the long arms swinging from a trunk, the backside of which stuck out as though (it was an irreverent colleague who said it; policemen are a wicked lot) he had a banana stuck up his jacksie. No more like a gorilla than would be your average gorilla, dressed up for tea with David Attenborough, brother of the *Gandhi* man.

He'd expected to find more customers in the pub, because access to it was not limited to the bridge end of the quay where the policemen stood guard. You could come in by a slip street from the little streets around, but it seemed that nobody had bothered. Last night, of course, and through the early morning was when the fireworks took place. By now, anybody who wanted to look upon the smoking, steaming ruin had done so, and moved on. Not much attraction in dull black, tottering walls to those who ran out into the streets to watch the real fun.

No, they hadn't tarted it. Not so you could notice. The same sagging beams, the same bar, the same settle by an inadequate fireplace. Even the bottles on shelves behind the counter looked the same. The same fusty smell of old beer and fag-ends left to burn away in ashtrays. But where old Ted Oatie used to stand behind his beer-engine stood now a very large lady with one of those bosoms that seems to have been fashioned in one enormous piece, come up like a bolster across the ribcage.

There was a crone, sitting on that settle with a glass of Guinness on the table pairing with it as it always had. She cackled as the inspector came in, crying in a shrill voice with cracks and a quaver in it: "Begob, 'tis himself! Oh, bejasus, 'tis the bloody man himself!"

"Hrrmph," said Inspector Rosher, unsmiling. "How do?" Who was this, then, who cackled at him with one tooth only, and that a black mandible?

"He doesn't know me," the crone cried in high delight. "Does he? Hasn't changed much, has he, but will you look at the hat? Nellie O'Hara it is. You won't have forgotten the Widow O'Hara?"

Bloody hell. Nellie O'Hara? Fighting head of a fighting clan. Not big, but solid as the dumpling flung by an Irish housewife into an Irish stew, all claws and teeth and fists and spitting fury when you took her in for knees-upping where it stopped the traffic, or punching up a Mrs. O'Cassidy in here, too many Guinnesses taken; Barney Dancey watching your back, truncheon drawn against rescue by her silver-tongued and meaty-fisted brood, or any other Irishman who chanced to be present. Including Mrs. O'Cassidy. Nellie O'Hara, the proud and the terrible, shrunk to this gray-seamed, cackling crone? Oh Christ—Christ—he could feel his own bones dwindling. Retirement loomed, and he was old.

"Nellie O'Hara," he said. "Well, well, well."

"Where's your lovely friend?"

"What friend?"

"Te odder feller. Lovely feller, te one who used to use his truncheon."

Barney. She meant Barney Dancey. "Back at the station." In the glassed-in reception office where he spent his days entering things into books, marking up the little people on bail when they reported in, dealing with the public and paper. He even knew how to work the bloody computer. And he, too was old, retiring in two or three years time.

"Are yez on yer own, den?" She'd lost none of the brogue. The Irish voice never sheds its rich color, even thinned down to a cracked tin bell. "Begob dere wuz a toime when ye'd never have done dat, coming arount here on yer own. Dey roide around now, in dere little black and white motorcars. It's not te same ting at all. Where did ye get te hat? It's not te same ting as yer helmet. Had dat off ye once or twoice, so Oi did." She wheezed and cackled happily, lifting the glass. It clinked on her solo tooth.

Perhaps it was the shock of seeing her grown so old, of having this ancient frailty suddenly superimposed on the image that flashed when she spoke her name. Perhaps the shaking of his old image of himself held him back from barking, or using the tone of patronizing avuncularity used by policemen toward their little regular bent. Not that you ever patronized Nellie O'Hara, or her brood, or come to that any of the Irish down this way. Nor were they bent, within the meaning. They rarely stole, there was not a pervert among them, they never went aburgling. They fought, that's all. Quite gently, as he crossed to the bar he said: "So you did, Nellie. So you did. Well, well. How's all the family?" And to the bolstered lady: "Half of bitter. And a pie."

"Blooming, tanks be to God. Except Danny. He's dead, may te saints keep his poor soul."

"Still up to the old tricks?" Which one was Danny?

"Ach, toimes isn't ohwat tey phwas. It's te National Assistant, tey all got dere telly now, and te little motorcars. Dey got married, all settled down. Te more kids ye have, te more ye get, 'tis a great system. Oi'm wishing tey'd had it win Oi wuz having one ivery year of me loife. Himself was a randy old divil when he had a few taken, ontil he fell in te canal. Eleven of 'em, he left me wid. Ye'll remember."

He remembered all right. Pushed to it, and given a quiet minute, he could probably have plucked all the names out of sighing memory. He'd run most of them in, some time or other. The morning after Christmas, or any Bank Holiday, or St. Patrick's Day—particularly St. Patrick's Day—they lined up in court with the Cassidys and Callahans, black-eyed, thick-lipped, swollen-knuckled, silver-tongued, and oddly ill at ease, wearing their Sunday suits; good Catholic boys all, ashamed now for what they had done, and would do again for sure almost as soon as they had paid the five-bob fine. But the women never apologized—this one and her sisters, her aunts, her daughters, they never apologized. They stood and glared, and their lovely voices accused the police of starting it all. But never, never did they use the common whore's avowal of sexual molestation—and they called the beak "Your Honor" with a kind of truculent dignity.

The old lady was speaking now. "Now Oi've got Oi couldn't tell you how many grandchildren. Oi may have *great* grandchildren, but Oi can't remember. Oi remember you, though. *And* te odder feller, wit te truncheon. Hard men, ye wuz. Very hard men." She cackled again. "Ah, but tey wuz happy days."

One name came to him, her youngest. The girl—Mavourneen—grown to about fourteen years old when he left. Pretty, judged within the wrinkled-stockinged saggy-skirted context of the family female line. Breasts grown to pert little apples, a wag to the bum when she walked. Mavourneen. "What happened to Mavourneen?"

A new cackle, and the crone wrinkled like a walnut. "He

doesn't know her! Hee hee hee. He doesn't know her.''

The bolster-bosomed woman had been nursing a secret sort of smile. She delivered his pint now, and placed a pie beside it. Not, alas, the smoking, juice-oozing pie of yesteryear, but the plastic-wrapped pink meat–stuffed horror of a latter day. Her voice came soft and beautiful. ''I'm Mavourneen. How are you, Mr. Rosher?''

Christ. She was middle-aged! It couldn't be! Those perky little tits, they couldn't have turned into that bloody great sad sack; the little waggy bum could never have spread so far. But something of the girl was there all right, when you looked: the eyes, the nose, the black and curly Irish hair. ''Well, I'll be damned,'' he said. And added, because he was disconcerted into saying something more, ''How long have you been working here?''

''Since Joseph went,'' she said. Her mother piped up: ''Fell off te back of a lorry.''

He'd known a lot of things fall off the back of a lorry, but not many people. Who would Joseph be? ''Ah,'' he said. ''Any kids?''

''None,'' said the bolstered woman; and again the old crone piped.

''She wuz te one who couldn't have any. God knows she tried. Many a toime before she was marrit, Oi had to take me hand to her.''

''Uh-huh,'' said Rosher. ''Well, well, well.''

''Hush up, Mother,'' the lady said. ''You're giving away me little secrets.''

''Hee hee hee,'' the old lady went. ''But she's a good girl, she wouldn't see her old mother want for a dhrop of Guinness. Will ye be buying me a half pint now, Mr. Rosher, for te old toime's sake?''

A notoriously frugal man, Rosher had worked out already how he would shift the price of his pint and the terrible pie clinging soggily to his big beige teeth onto the expenses chit, but his calculations did not include buying half pints for extraneous crones. Buy her one, he'd have to buy one for the daughter. And O'Haras didn't stop at one. ''Ah,'' he said; and was saved by the entry of one of the uniform policemen who had been guarding the slope down to the quay. The policeman said: "I think you ought to have a look at what they've found, Mr. Rosher."

Rosher turned, grateful for the interruption. "What who's found, lad?"

"The fire fellers. It's a body." The policeman was so shaken up, he added, "Sir."

2

A charred body is not a pretty sight. This one was gone beyond recognition. The firemen had brought it out and laid it as neatly as it could be laid beside one of the fire appliances. Station Officer Faith stood with it, together with a common or garden fireman. The senior man said when Rosher arrived, not waiting to be asked, "In the basement. We've gone in, routine check to make sure nothing's going to flare up again."

"Uh-huh." They were each other's kind of man. Professionals, neither inclined to circumlocution. Thus, the man kept back to await the inspector's arrival had to be the man who came upon the ugly thing. No need even to ask the question. The policeman merely waggled an eyebrow. The fireman said, promptly: "Close in by the wall."

"Uh-huh." Rosher turned to his constable. "Been onto the station?"

"From the car," the constable said. "My oppo'll have done it by now."

"Uh-hnn. Do they know I'm down here?"

"He'll have told 'em."

"Make sure he has. Tell 'em I'll hang on."

Away went the policeman, along the cobbles and back to the slope. Inspector Rosher stood beside the firemen. Nobody said anything for some time. The man still played his hose downward from his appliance ladder, steam still billowing up, but the others had finished spraying through the door. The common or garden fireman said at last: "D'you want me any more?"

The senior fireman turned a querying eye to Rosher, who responded: "No. So long as I can get hold of you if I need you."

"I'll be around," the man said. He walked away in his great shiny thigh boots to rejoin his mates.

A further short silence. The senior fireman indicated the body with a small nod of the helmet. "Tramp?" he said.

"Probably," said Rosher. "Wino. Dropout." All sorts of possibilities, really. He'd never known an abandoned warehouse where small malpractices were not taking place among the drifting homeless, the darkness-seeking perverts, the glue-sniffing young, and the rarer—in a small town—junkie come with a rush to the gutter. One of them probably set it on fire without meaning to. This one got left, probably stoned blind and unnoticed when the others scrambled. Unless the owner did it, for the insurance. He spoke again.

"Who owns it?"

Again the fireman's helmet inclined, this time toward the sparely angular modern building separated from the wrecked warehouse by a wide passage, almost a yard in itself, along which the haulage trucks passed to the yard and maintenance garage at the back. "Same bloke who owns that."

"Nore-Smith?" The ex-mayor.

"Nore-Smith." A minute of shared rumination, then the fireman spoke again. "It wouldn't have been insured for much."

Professionals, you see, think upon the same things, and can refer to the other man's thinking with complete and economical confidence. Many a man has burned his warehouse down for the sake of the insurance. This one would be chancing the new building too, of course, right next door; but then, in a time of rising truck-running costs and general recession, to lose them both might have suited him well, premiums all paid up.

"Has he been down?"

"He's away. Staff came in. I sent 'em all home."
"Uh-huh."
More silence, until a police car came, nosing down among the hoses; and then a black car containing the doctor without whose pronouncement that it is indeed dead no body may be removed, unless it is holding up traffic flow; and finally the hearse from the hospital, to take the poor, black, shriveled thing to the final indignity of slab and postmortem, and probably a vagrant's unwept-over grave. It happens to be a surprising number of people, year in, year out. Nobody emerged from the pub to see what was going on.

When Inspector Rosher got back to the station, he went in through the front entrance rather than by the unobtrusive CID door at the back, so that he could pause at the window of the glassed reception office for a word with the incumbent. He said: "Made a right mess of one of the old warehouses, Barney."

Sergeant Barney Dancey. A good man. Truly, happy faith still in his unblighted soul. And this after thirty-odd years in a police force. Such men, surely, when death has closed the bonny blue eyes, are wafted straight to the very highest cumulus, there to strum their golden harps. "So they tell me," he said. "Been down there?"

He knew Rosher had been down there, the radio call when the body was discovered said he was there, and not a sparrow fell in this station but Barney, in his little glazed and varnished-oak office, heard the plonk and wove it into the overall picture. People asked Barney all sorts of things. He usually had the answers.

"Uh-huh," said Inspector Rosher. "Just got back. Gutted. Changed a lot, round that way."

"Yeah. Quieter, too, since our time. We don't get a lot of trade from that area, nowadays. I think the council estates have depressed them. And then, they've got the telly. Time they've watched *Coronation Street* and *Crossroads,* they haven't got time to lush up for a punch-up."

"I saw old Widow Nellie. In the Ring o' Roses."

Barney grinned. His teeth were much neater, much whiter than

Rosher's, but then they were much newer. He'd had them barely eighteen months. "That figures. How is she?"

"I didn't recognize her. And you remember the youngest—Mavourneen?"

"The pretty one." He could have said the prettiest one. Not a bad-looking family by any means, those O'Haras, if you looked under the slop, though tending in the old days to get somewhat spoiled by broken noses or a sudden paucity of front teeth due to colliding them abruptly with a fist.

"She's serving in the bar now. Begod, she's put on a bit of weight."

"She would, Alf, she would. Thirty years of feeding since we knew her. It's the praties that does it."

"She's been married and widowed. Husband fell off the back of a lorry."

"What was she married to, then, a telly set?"

Very, very rarely did the grim and, some said, grisly mouth of Inspector Rosher curve beneath the black hat into a grin. When it did, as often as not it was under the benign influence of Barney, best oppo he ever had and the only one with whom he had worked without friction. "She didn't say. Who owns the pub now?"

Barney could answer this straight off the cuff. He knew the name and track record of every licensee in town. "An Edwin Chafers. Old Oatie died, long time ago. The old lady went to her sister, Wolverhampton as I recall. Think it was Wolverhampton. The Chafers used to have the Dun Cow, out Wapley way." Wapley is a village. And a pretty one, too.

"Do they have any trouble?" Little punch-ups, unless they result in grievous bodily or even death, do not come within the operational sphere of the CID officer. Rosher did not recall hearing anything of the pub at all since he left the area.

"Not even an after-hours sip at the Guinness. Unless the beat lads wink at it a little, like we used to. Couple of 'em—O'Flaherties, Callahans—we've had in for D and D, but things ain't what they used to be." D and D is drunk and disorderly, and Barney was smiling the soft smile of fond remembrance. It sat rather well on him. ''Flipping time's flown, hasn't it? Seems like yesterday.''

''Aye,'' said Rosher.

''The bloody O'Haras. Well, well, well.''

Rosher began to move on. ''See you, Barney.''

''See you, Alf.'' The only man in all the station—the only man in all the world—who called the inspector Alf. First names are bandied without shame between policemen, constable and sergeant, sergeant and inspector, inspector and superintendent, until you scale the ultimate pinnacle where squats the Old Man, the Chief Constable, Commander, or equivalent, whom lesser men call sir. But Rosher, referred to out of his presence as Old Blubbergut, was addressed directly as Inspector, or as Mr. Rosher. Never by first name.

When he reached his office, the inspector hung his black hat above the battleship-gray raincoat on the peg provided, and sat down at his desk. He typed with mumbled swearing—the damn machine had a habit of going &9@¾''9%⅞—his report of the finding of the body, time of its removal to the morgue, and so on. Bare details, which would marry in with the fuller report of the fire officer, who must send the lot all clipped together with photos of the body itself and area where found to the Home Office, copies retained for himself and supplied to the police. This done, he ate an Eccles cake and drank bitumen-black tea in the upstairs canteen, then came back to tackle the hated paperwork that plagues every policeman from the day he pilots his new-issue boots out of the station for his first beat shift until he emerges finally, wearing his civvy hat to hide the scalp poking through his thinning hair and clutching a gold watch.

He was wondering whether to go home for an hour before setting out for that doorway where he would lurk awaiting the arrival of little bent men with a jimmy, or whether to ascend again to the canteen for a pie and chips, let somebody else do the washing up, when the summons came. Would he go up, please, to the Chief Constable's office.

Pausing only to lick his fingers for better smoothing above the ears of the short back and sides haircut, and to make sure no tuft stuck up at the back below the tenpenny-piece–size pink tonsure let into the crown, he came forth to clunk along the passage that clacked before they put the composition flooring down over the bare stone; up stairs upon which, at the level where superintendents worked, the compo gave way to cocoanut matting; and up again to where even this refinement was considered ill-suited to the hand-tooled brogues of the Chief Constable, who dwelt alone on carpet in a beautifully paneled office having the benefit of a fine mahogany desk, a picture of Robert Peel on the wall, and an uninterrupted view of the parking lot.

Doubling the Mighty Hammer that had laid many a man cross-eyed and twitching on the ring floor, and a plenitude of malefactors in less orthodox locations, he knocked his hairy knuckles against the door. "Enter," cried the very top man in the pecking order.

In went Rosher. Two men were with the Chief Constable, who sat at his fine desk looking urbane, as a man in his position is entitled to do. One was a Detective Superintendent Ernie Fisk, a bulky man of few words and some of those not in front of the ladies; the other, Chief Superintendent Rolli Rawlins, head under God of the Uniform Branch.

The Chief Constable said: "Ah. Mr. Rosher. Come in, come in. You found a body today, I believe? The warehouse fire."

"I did, sir," said Rosher. "Well, that is to say, the firemen did. I supervised its removal. My report should be with you by now." His voice was tinged suddenly with the oddly mangled telephone accent that came upon him when he conversed with men who possessed cultured vocal tone, or a hyphenated surname (he once interviewed a baronet who never understood a word he said), or a whole stack of money and clout; and female members (respectable) of the general public.

"Yes, yes," the Chief Constable said. "I have it here." It lay on his leather-bound blotter with the Algerian gold whirly bits all round the edge. His wife had brought it back from a cruise, together with a camel saddle. "You know that area well, I believe?"

"It was my first beat, sir. It's changed a lot, of course, since then."

"Mm. Yes. Well, it would, of course. I have the postmortem report here. Apparently your body's skull was shattered."

"Ah. Falling brickwork, beams? The building was gutted."

"The wall protected him, it seems. I've been onto the fire brigade, they say he was huddled against it. Not pinned down or anything, what little timber wasn't burned away was further in."

"Ah. Hmm."

The Chief Constable read on into the postmortem report, holding it in the lily-white hands with the beautifully manicured nails. Half-moons like little Turkish scimitars. "Absence of carbon particles in the lungs, no sign of carbon monoxide in the blood. Traces of fat embolism in the lungs." He glanced up at Rosher, inviting reaction. All present seemed to be inviting reaction, as senior men in these circumstances will, having nothing better to do.

"Uh-huh," said Rosher. Bodies are common enough in the life of a policeman; but except when the occasional crashed car flames, burned ones are very rare. He did not know the clinical significance of the summarized forensic details. But he knew well enough what the Chief Constable was adding up to. "Murder?"

"Let us say," the chief said, "that the subject was almost certainly dead before the fire got him. Mr. Fisk is going down to see what there is to see. I would like you to go with him." In fact, it is your familiarity with the area and its people that has laid the matter onto Fisk, rather than onto Fillimore. If we get the body identified rapidly and it turns out to be a local, you should know the family at least, who to go to and where to find them, for all his background details. With Fisk, you work well enough. Put you with Percy Fillimore, you both give ninety percent of your mental capacity to abrading each other. Pains in the sacroiliac, you are; so I give you Fisk.

"Uh-huh," said Rosher. "I've got a stunt tonight."

"Hand it over."

"Right." Right indeed. The potential for kudos comes with murder. A very rare tidbit, murder. And Ernie Fisk. Fisk was all right. Anybody was all right, so long as it was not Chief Superintendent (Percy) Fillimore, the bastard. Inspector Rosher's hairy hand went to the pocket of his blue serge trousers, came out with a crumpled grayish handkerchief that would have been ironed into snow-white creases in the days before the fat wife went home weeping to Mother. The men braced.

"Oh, Christ," said Detective Superintendent Ernie Fisk. "Take cover."

"Pardon?" said Inspector Rosher, and raised the handkerchief to wide and hairy nostrils.

3

They drove first to the mortuary, to cast a fresh eye on the corpse, carved now, too black and shriveled to tell them anything, and to speak with the pathologist who dealt with the postmortem. It really did look like murder. The pathologist said so, no messing. By the time the two policemen emerged into the soft evening, both were thinking of the matter as murder.

Normally, after the discovery of a body dead in off-color circumstances, the surrounding area is roped off and thick with policemen, many of whom look more like public urinal graffiti poets, or men from the Water Board who must never, never be let into the house without official identification, or men who sleep for preference on mattresses stuffed with prime horse dung, purveying it to gardeners who have lost faith in ICI. Some, since policemen get younger all the time, resemble the secondary modern scholar who, having nutted Sir in the choppers, has taken to the hills and slept rough ever since. A motley crew. And very clever.

They are Scenes of Crime men, Forensic Squad men, Drugs Squad men, if drugs feature; about whom, even the others say "Yuck." "Well, sod it," they retort hotly, "you cannot infiltrate and get close to junkies looking as though you were got by a multiple tailor out of one of those lady dummies that stand, in these happy times, bare-breasted in store windows, drawing the wistful eye of men who wish their wives still looked like that.'' Specialists all, these unlikely lads. Where would we be without them?

But down at the canal basin, when Fisk and Rosher arrived, were none of these men. This was not your normal discovery, it was not even officially murder. These two were here to grab a flying start should fuller examination prove conclusively the necessity for a murder investigation. As it would, no doubt. But it hadn't as yet.

There was one fire engine left now, stationed by the burned-out building, and only one guardian policeman. A barrier had been erected at the bottom of the slope down from the bridge to the cobbled quay, and a huge truck was stopped just short of it. The driver, high up in his cab, leaned from the open window to address the lone policeman, who had walked up from his place in front of the warehouse.

As the two ranking officers came within earshot, the driver was saying: ''How am I supposed to offload, then? I got a full truck here.''

''Sorry, mate,'' the policeman said. ''That's your worry. You can't go in, they're afraid the walls are going to collapse.''

''Sod that.'' The driver was turning truculent. Tired, probably, he'd have been driving all day. ''When did it happen?''

''In the night. Went up like November the Fifth.''

''Where's Bert, then?''

''Who's Bert?''

''The bloody foreman.''

''Oh. He's coming.''

He was. An overalled, roly-poly little man, hurrying out from the wide entrance to the haulage-firm yard. Fisk and Rosher passed on, nodding to the constable as they went by. Let him sort it out, no business of theirs.

The Ring o' Roses was open for custom, Rosher noticed. No reason why it should not be, it stood well away from danger, no matter how or when the warehouse walls fell down. Several people sat on the bench built along the pleasant facade, and more at two little tables brought out to offer the punter full benefit of this mellow weather. They sat with their drinks, hoping for something to happen. There was nothing much on the telly. The small boats had been moved from the private moorings too close to the black walls, and were tied now aft of the Happy Wanderer narrowboats, between the warehouse and the pub. Nothing else seemed to have changed since the inspector was here earlier. Fisk said: "Well—the Old Man sent us down to look at it. I suppose we'd better look at it."

"Uh-huh," said Inspector Rosher. They had come to a halt in front of the warehouse. Beyond the barrier the truck was in motion now, backing carefully up the slope with the roly-poly foreman walking backward behind it, signaling to help the driver with the sharp turn he must make to bring his great vehicle onto the road again. The policeman stood on the road, ready to flag down approaching traffic. There was none, but he would be right in the steaming heap if some goon came flying along and went womp into the unexpected back of a bloody great articulated eight-wheeler. The inspector, moving forward toward the gap where the warehouse door had been, indicated with a tilt of the black hat the smart modern building set back next door. "He was lucky. Has he been down yet? Nore-Smith?"

Snap judgment might condemn this as a question directed daftly at a man who, since he was assigned to the job at the same time as the questioner, could not be expected to have the answer. But talk had taken place in the Chief Constable's office before Rosher arrived. Fisk would have the fuller picture. He said now: "Holiday. Continent. Flying back."

Another man who suited Rosher well, with his terse professsional method of communication. They advanced until they stood in the warehouse doorway. Nothing of obvious use to them inside. Just a tangle of carbonized beams and the remains of interior walls that collapsed to let the roof fall in. Everything cooling now, soggy with the firemens' chemical-impregnated water. They stood and gazed a while. Fisk said: "Found over there. By the wall. Not much point in going in, everything destroyed. Suggest we visit the pub, see if anybody's been sleeping rough in here."

They turned away, nodding as they moved toward the pub to the fire crew standing idly by their engine. Rosher spoke.

"Who owns it?" Nore-Smith, the fireman had said. He could have been wrong.

"The warehouse? Nore-Smith. Bought the two of 'em before the council moved in and took the rest over."

"Wouldn't be going for the insurance, would he?"

"Couldn't have been insured for much."

"The site?" Quite commonly, a site is worth considerably more than the building encumbering it. If the building is listed, a good way to evade the order is to burn it out of the way, or pay a bunch of herberts to remove lead from the roof (they will flog it as a perk) and make holes in the roof itself, so that in a year or two—during which your site value should increase—you may truthfully claim that vandalism and foul weather have made the building unsafe, and so obtain permission to pull it down. All you need then is planning permission, granted almost as a formality, to rebuild on the site. Nice little investment, sometimes. Better than a Building Society.

"Wouldn't be worth a lot, these days." Fisk produced his baccy pouch and began to stuff the pipe that seldom left his mouth. Substitute nipple. Well, that's what the psychologists say. "Five years ago, maybe. Recession's done for that, nobody's building. And it's a conservation area now. White elephant. Council'll probably offer him a few bob for it, bring the lot under Leisure and Environmental control."

"Uh-huh. Could have wanted the space, extend his truck-parking area."

"Wouldn't allow it, would they? It's going to be a proper little Venice down here. They might mock up a Doge's Palace on it, that's about all, charge it to the rates. Bigger and better white elephant." The pipe was lit, and drawing nicely.

Policemen, even as other men, pay rates. Fisk had no love for his. Nor had Rosher. He said, scathingly, "Huh," and they walked on toward the pub.

Mavourneen was outside with a tray, delivering a pint or two and collecting empty glasses, by her presence inviting fresh orders before she went back in. She had certainly put on weight with the years, and yet the effect was not entirely unattractive. Apart from the bolster bosom, which must surely have been hauled by muscle-power into its veritable hammock, the flesh bloomed cleanly, cuddled the bones without sagging. Incredibly, she must be in the late forties. Bloody hell, thought Rosher.

She stood with her tray until the policemen came up, when she said in the soft-edged brogue: "Good evening, Mr. Rosher. A fine one it is."

"'Evening," said Rosher. Should he call her Mavourneen? Too chummy. And he didn't know her widow-name. "Mm. Yes. Grand."

"Will you be wanting a drink?"

"Not now. Never on duty." Not with senior rank present.

"Are you on duty, then? What about your friend?"

Hesitation from Fisk; and then he said: "No." It came almost abruptly. A repudiation, the brave refusal to embrace temptation. Mr. Fisk had a drinking problem. It was an open secret that nobody recognized officially. It had never affected his work, he never roared in the street or punched policemen.

"This is Superintendent Fisk," said Rosher.

"How d'you do." Mavourneen smiled at the superintendent with her Irish-blue eyes. "And are you both down here on the business of the poor feller? The one in the fire."

Fisk made a reply. "We are. Wondered if you can help us. Has anybody been sleeping rough in there, do you know? Any tramps, winos? Anybody going in and out?"

"Haven't seen anybody. But I go home at night, I'm only here opening hours. Mr. and Mrs. Chafers may know. Will you come in and see them now?"

The people sitting around were eyeing the policemen curiously, ears obviously agape to hear what was being said. As he moved forward with Superintendent Fisk to follow the broad back of Mavourneen into the pub, Rosher's hard little eyes darted among them.

Nobody that he knew, so far as he knew. Some of 'em might have been in short trousers when he was down here. Sod it, some of their *fathers* might have been in short trousers. He might have put back their very conception for a few years by routing out those fathers from the dark corners where they experimented with giggling kids who by now could be—would be, if their daughters inherited their precocity—grandmothers. Over there, whispering together, were two men, one losing youth but the other very pretty, who would never need rousting out from traffic with naughty young ladies. And that was legal now, if you didn't flash it in public. Bloody hell. He'd run a few of *them* in, in his time.

The Widow O'Hara was among those present in the pub, sitting in the same place she had occupied when he was here this afternoon. She cackled at him now and raised her glass in a gaily mocking salute, the saucy old bat. He nodded back, iron-faced for two reasons: he did not like sauciness from anybody, most certainly not from crones who'd disturbed a terrible lot of the peace in their day; and sure as eggs, one jot or tittle of encouragement and she'd be after him for a Guinness.

Mr. Chafers had a belly and was middle-aged, a strangely Victorian man with a black, drooping mustache and grayed hair brushed into the Olde Tyme Music Hall barman's quiff. He bore the marks of long-term toping, and whereas most people meeting Inspector Rosher for the first time tended to find themselves somewhat riveted, his melancholy eye focused more sharply on Superintendent Fisk. The superintendent carried his stigmata more subtly. It showed only in a certain rubicundity spread across the broad face, an almost innocent quality in the light blue eyes. But you can't beat a toping landlord when it comes to cutting sign.

Mr. Chafers had seen nobody moving in, out, or round about the warehouse. Nor had his wife, standing small, snap-eyed, and black-haired beside him behind the bar. "Mind you," he said, "they could get in at the back, couldn't they? From the street. You wouldn't see 'em from down here." "That's right," his wife said. "Wouldn't see 'em at all." No, they said, they didn't know what went on in any of the buildings, they didn't stop up all night watching, did they? When the pub closed, they went to bed. Didn't even know there was a fire until the engines woke them up. Would you care for a little something, before you go?

No, the policemen said. Very nice of you (Fisk said this), but no, thank you. The Widow O'Hara waved and bared her tooth merrily at Rosher as they moved out.

Dusk was in the offing by now, the yellow lamp upon the bridge switched on and reflected in the still water, the September moon rising like a cheese. People were drinking up and leaving as the small chill of evening advanced, but the two poufs still sat on, glasses of gin, or it could have been vodka, set before them.

Inspector Rosher said: "What now?"

"Back to the station, I reckon," said Fisk. "Can't do much until we get it as murder official."

They walked back along the quay, up the slope to where they had left the car, well short of the bridge where the road was wide enough for parking to cause no obstruction. Policemen are careful about things like that. The great truck had been taken into the narrow street running between the warehouses, where it did cause obstruction, filling the space so that nothing but a bicycle, and that with narrow handlebars, could have squeezed past. But what the heck, nobody used that road. Where was there to go? Through a gate set in the terminating wall and into the haulage yard, that's all.

The driver of the truck was in the small yard office, saying to the foreman: "We can't leave it there all night, nobody to guard it."

"Can't stay here all night, can we? They only let me stay to see you in."

"There's fucking coppers all over the place."

"Only one. And he's in front of the warehouse."

"Them two that went down—they're coppers."

"Well, we can't start mucking it about now, can we? We can't get all them washing machines out all on our tod, can we? Out there? And then start getting the sodding floor up? It'll *have* to stay there till we can run it in in the morning, offload with the lads in the usual way. Then I can send you out empty. We'll have to find somewhere else to store the gear."

"If we're fucking here in the morning. If we ain't in the nick."

"We'll be in the sodding nick if we start mucking it about."

"Who was the geezer they found dead in there, then?"

"I don't know, do I? Nobody does. There was a geezer in there, that's all I know." The blue pungency of foreign tobacco wafted around the smart little transport office. Both men were smoking. Gaulloise. Most of the firm smoked Continental brands, brought back by the drivers from their trips to France and Belgium and the Netherlands. In those and other EEC countries are firms where the personnel smoke only English brands, bought duty free on the way back from making the run in reverse. There's a certain cachet about it. The birds seem to like it. A foreign fag, a leather jacket, a tousled head, and muscle enough to pilot a great diesel truck up and down the Continent—that's macho.

"So, we make nap-all out of the last lot?" This driver was quite big, and tousle-haired, and he had a leather jacket. So he was macho, although married and not on peak at present. He looked tired, as truck drivers do in the evening, and fretful with the glowering fret of the man who prefers to solve problems with muscle rather than brain.

"I keep telling you, don't I?" Roly-poly little Bert had no macho at all. Bert Humsey. Even the name lacks it, whatever "it" may be, and you would never have thought him big enough to get behind the wheel of one of those huge trucks and see through the windshield to drive it. But drive he could, better than any—you should have seen him back his eight-wheelers into spaces almost narrower than they were, without a flake off the paint—and but for his mechanical genius, half the macho boys with the muscle would have been off the road, or phoning back all the time from breakdowns, crying for help. Happy this firm that engaged him six months ago, to replace one Ted Hoylake, killed in a car crash. "I keep telling you, don't I? The bloody lot went up. Dead loss, we gotta count it out."

"Fuck it," the driver said.

"Count yourself lucky," Bert told him. "If they'd found it there, we *would* have been in the shit. And we'd better get out of here, before they start wondering what we're up to."

"Fuck it," the driver said again. "I could use a drink."

"I'll buy you one. Ring o' Roses. We can sit outside, keep an eye on things till closing time."

"That's a lot of help," said the driver.

The two policemen did not make the trip back to the station. They never even started on it. They had driven down in Fisk's own car, but before they had time to board it, having both front doors open to permit their ducking in, the guardian constable came charging up the slope from the quay, signaling wildly. They slammed the doors and walked back to meet him. He cried as he came: "Message from the station, sir. They can't raise you."

Fisk glanced at Inspector Rosher. Inspector Rosher dug into the durable blue serge suit and produced his personal radio. Flicked the switch. Held it to his hairy ear. Shook it. Held it to his other ear. "On the blink," he said.

That—and Rosher always said so—is the trouble with all these bloody gadgets, computers, and radar and radios and the rest of 'em. The more you get, the more you have to go wrong. We got along all right without them, he said, in the old days. Better clearing rate than we've got now. Strangely, perhaps because gadgets know well enough who hates them and react resentfully, those that he was forced to deal with directly—his personal radio, the electric typewriter—often went on the blink and were inclined to smoke. And Fisk, as upper brass, never carried a walkie-talkie. As the queen never carries money. Wherever he walked, a lesser man would tell him when he was wanted. Without comment, he stretched out a hand now. The constable handed over his own little oblong box. When the superintendent pressed the switch, it squawked as God intended it to do.

All three men heard what it said. It said that the case was being treated now officially as murder. It said that Superintendent Fisk and Inspector Rosher were to stay there, awaiting the arrival of the

Chief Constable and all those scruffy men who would be arriving soon, in force. It said that dental records had established identity of the body—already. That was smart work. It was John Patrick O'Hara, aged twenty, of 15 Jubilee Street. Message ends.

Superintendent Fisk strangled the cackling static with his thumb and handed the set back to the constable, cocking a light blue eye at Rosher. That man knew what he was asking. He said:

"O'Hara. Big family, used to give us a bit of trouble in the old days. Punch-ups, D and D, nothing big. The old girl sitting in the pub, she's one of 'em. So's the big woman, the one we were talking to."

"Uh-hnn," said the superintendent. "Better get back there, eh? You can go and have a word with them. I'll hang about the warehouse, wait for the Old Man."

4

They all walked together down the slope, back to the warehouse area where Superintendent Fisk stayed with the uniform constable while Inspector Rosher moved on, to where the lights were showing now in the Ring o' Roses bar, and the drinkers who had elected to stay outside nearly all gone. The two poufs sauntered by as he approached, making for the way out from the canal basin at this end by the slip street leading into the estates. They eyed the powerful, peculiarly apelike figure with interest; but not with the interest they would have shown, moved back to the generation of thirty years ago, when not all the fluttering lashes wafted toward the barrel-chested boxer were attached to women. Two men emerging from the haulage yard checked momentarily when they saw him, before the roly-poly one said: "Come on. He's only going to the pub."

"What for?"

"How do I know? They probably lash 'em out free beer."

They followed, some distance back from the inspector, who found Mavourneen just coming out of the pub door carrying a tray. By the time he reached her, she was gathering empty glasses from one of the tables.

When it came to breaking news of bereavement, and presumably she was among the bereaved, since all the O'Haras were related, Rosher was not the ideal choice for the job. By nature reinforced with a lifetime of training, he kept his own emotions so deeply hidden that few people guessed that he had any. Emotion in other people embarrassed him. So without even realizing that it gave him the aspect of an ill-intentioned gorilla, he fixed her with grim little eyes from under the black hat-brim and said sternly: "Ah. Mm. The body. Found in the fire. It's been identified."

Still couldn't rake up a name to address her by, this overblown and widowed version of a child he knew.

She straightened up from the table. "Have you now?" The brogue came sweetly from her. "We'd heard the poor feller was so badly burned nobody could put a name to him."

"Dental records," he said. The haulage-firm men had caught up by now. They were passing by. "His—er—name. O'Hara. John Patrick O'Hara."

He thought for a moment that she was going to fall down. Good job she had not picked up the tray with the glasses on it; the whole lot would have smashed and shattered on the cobbles. The dusking light hid the changing color of her face but her eyes widened, one hand went for support to the table, the other rose to the solid buttress of her breast. "Holy Mary," she whispered. "Mother of God."

"He—er—I imagine you will know the next of kin." The haulage-firm men had seated themselves on the bench along the pub facade. They were looking this way. Hearing every word, no doubt about that. A policeman more suited to this delicate branch of the business would have eased her into privacy before he slapped it on her.

"Me . . . me brother," she said.

"Ah. Which one?" There was a bloody great packet of 'em.

"Shaun. He's . . . he went to Australia. Wid Mary. John's been . . . living with me. In my house. With me. And me mother."

"Ah." Me mother. The Widow O'Hara. Two Widow O'Haras, near enough, living in the one house. A small council house, 15 Jubilee Street. That could be a jolly ménage, especially if this young John Patrick had come up true to the family pattern. Mary, presumably, was the boy's mother. "The address. In Australia. Do you have it?"

"It'll be at home. Somewhere." The plump-fingered hand had left the bosom to tinker with her hair. Sooner or later, a woman will turn to the hair in times of stress. "How . . . how did he? . . . What was he doing in there?"

"We don't know. But we're treating it as murder."

On the bench the two haulage men twitched, the big one starting as though to rise to his feet. The roly-poly one restrained him with a hand. Nobody noticed. "Murder?" she said. "Who'd . . . oh no . . . not. . . . Nobody would . . . Oh, how am I going to tell me mother? She tinks the world of Johnnie."

Again, your more gifted copper would have said he would do that for her. And ignore her use of the present tense, when Johnnie had gone into the past. It commonly takes a little time for people to adjust. The inspector made no offer. He said: "Hmmph. Well, I'm sorry we've had to. . . . We can offer you transport home." He glanced back toward the warehouse. Yes, transport was there. Lined up on the slope: two police cars and a small van. Men were moving in, the Chief Constable's fine limousine just arriving.

"No," she said. "No. It's—nice of you, but—we'll manage. Thank you."

"Well," he said, "we'll have to talk to you. If we run you home, we're there already."

"Ah yes," she said, just as if she were paying attention. "Yes. Of course."

"I'll—er—go and arrange it." He turned, to guide his boxy-toed shoes back to where there was transport.

She picked up the tray; and she did a thing that nobody would have expected who did not know that in shock, people more often than not cling to the normal to soften the impact of the abnormal. She paused where the two men were sitting, on her way back into the pub, and she said: "Can I get you anything?"

"Yes. Yes," said roly-poly Bert Humsey. "'Evening, Mavourneen. I'll have a pint of . . . no, I'll have a brandy." He glanced at his companion. "So will he."

"Make it a double," the driver said.

"Two doubles, dear," said roly-poly Bert.

She passed on into the bar. The driver hissed: "It was Johnnie O'Hara. It was Johnnie in the fucking fire."

Bert whispered back: "I know, I know, I know."

"Murdered, the fucking copper said."

"I know, I know. Maybe it wasn't murder—maybe it was an accident. They make a lot of cockups, the pigs, don't they?"

"Murder. Fuck that," said the driver. "I don't like fucking murder. They'll be hanging around all over the place, the pigs will."

As Rosher walked toward the men scattered about in front of the warehouse, they suddenly began to trot. Those on this side, Superintendent Fisk and the newly arrived uniform chief Rolli Rawlins among them, trotted this way. On the other side, men coming down from the cars checked, those closest to the building turning to trot that way back toward the slope. Only the firemen stood firm by their lone engine. The long, black wall seemed, when he looked at it, to be teetering. And suddenly, with a loud thundering rumble, it collapsed inward—as those cunning firemen knew it would, but didn't tell the police for fear of spoiling the giggle when they all trotted—leaving only about ten feet of itself still standing. That buggers it, the inspector thought.

He was perfectly right. Whatever was of use in there, if anything was—and that was very doubtful, fire being a great purger—was buried now under all those tons of brick and rubble. All those scruffy specialists, the Scene of Crime men, Forensic lads, even the photographer, could go home again. Nothing they could do here.

He walked on, to where Fisk and Rolli Rawlins and a few other men had regrouped. Fisk was repeating Rosher's thought, using almost identical words: "That's buggered that. We can all go home again."

"Could get it cleared, given time," Chief Superintendent Rawlins replied. Chiefs of the uniform branch have infinite confidence in the capacity of the force under their command. They do but give the order, and it is done. So they believe. Astonishingly, they turn out mostly to have been right.

"Not worth it," Fisk said. "Only ash and timber in there, this'll have bashed it all over the place. Lucky we didn't have anybody inside." Luck was not concerned, really. At the first sign that anybody intended to enter, the firemen would have stepped in at once. Forty lads all and of Rabelaisian humor, but they do not lurch about and slap their thighs as innocent policemen vanish beneath some tons of roaring rubble.

"Soon set a squad on."

"We need you lads for other things." House-to-house and the like. "Fire brigade can get onto that."

Rosher came up. He said: "The lad was living with the barmaid at the pub. Mavourneen O'Hara; he was her nephew. Thought I'd see her home. We'll have to go up there. Might as well do it now."

"Right," said Fisk. "We'll see to the house-to-house. Take one of the squad cars."

So Rosher went on along the collapsed warehouse frontage and up the slope, passing on the way the Chief Constable and all those men who had trotted backward, now in forward motion again. He commandeered a squad car and sat beside the uniform driver as it edged down past the groups and the fire engine to the Ring o' Roses. No other way to approach with that huge truck blocking the narrow back street, short of setting out to thread through the council housing.

Bert Humsey and his driver were the only drinkers left sitting outside the pub. Others were inside, but Rosher did not need to enter. As the car drew up Mavourneen came through the door, holding her mother by the arm. The outer Widow O'Hara undoubtedly had withered, but the inner seemed not to have shrunk. Her battered hat was askew, as he remembered it on many a Saturday night and at the close of Catholic celebration days, and she tugged against her daughter's hand, crying loud and furious: "Will you let go me arm now, ye daft biddy—will you be feeling the back of me hand? Oi haven't had enough to wet me whistle and it's not even closing toime."

She had not been told that one of her brood was dead. Rosher knew it. They love their Guinness, the Irish; but they love the family more. Had she known, it would have been the grandson she would have been skirling to Heaven over, not the Guinness. Mavourneen was handling her without difficulty, the threat of back-of-the-hand no longer supported by any substance. He got out of the car, not to render assistance but to open the back door, saying quite jovially: "Come on then, Nellie. Let's be having you inside."

A few she'd taken, nobody could doubt it, and probably Guinness and very old age lap together into confusion. She knew it was Rosher all right, and she knew he'd been away, so she wasn't all that far gone. She cried: "Jasus, te bloody man's only come back today, and he's knocking me off already. And hardly a dhrop gone past me lips."

Perhaps he, too, had jumped automatically back in time. It was so familiar. What Mavourneen was doing used to be done, with far greater difficulty, by himself or Barney. Certainly he used the tone, even the words, that he had used many, many times toward her, long long ago. Now he said: "Nobody's knocking you, Nellie."

"Mrs. Bloody O'Hara to you," she said, "you ugly great gorilla."

Now Rosher, fronting a mirror, did not see a gorilla. So when she called him one—and she always did, she always did—it in no way hit him hard. He took it now, as he took it then, as backhanded tribute to his masculine muscular force. It pleased him then. It pleased him now. Quite like old times; even to the way she ceased to struggle and protest as soon as she reached the car, and entered it to sit on the back seat quite demurely. Many D and D regular clients do this, God knows why. They seem to operate within a self-applied set of rules, as for a game. If the copper gets the player actually to the car, the player submits. Score the copper one.

It was not far, to Jubilee Street. Hardly worth commandeering the car for, but it is customary police courtesy not to turn distress adrift, letting it walk home. The street lay just behind the warehouse area, a short row of semidetached houses all exactly alike, as though the council architect, having produced one design, found himself burned out by it and had to be revived with a golden handshake and an inflation-proof pension. To save the ratepayer the cost of replacement, they duplicated his design all over these estates. Well, it was an improvement on the old squalor.

The Widow O'Hara raised no ruckus when they got her out of the car. She went peaceably, with Mavourneen holding her arm, up the concrete path and into the concrete house. A miserable material, concrete, but quite good enough for the poor. Inspector Rosher and his driver followed them in.

There were people about, and they looked across curiously; but tame people, with telly sets and middle-class aspirations insinuated into them by the box, and by the years of solid income, and by the magazines they were able to read nowadays, when hookey was the exception rather than the rule. All, all were gone, the giants of yesteryear. And here was the shrunken last of them, being toddled respectably home.

"Go into the lounge," said Mavourneen, when they were in the tiny hall. "I'll just get her to bed."

Lounge? There wasn't a lounge for miles around, in the old days.

"Oi'm not toired," the aged lady said. First protest since she entered the car.

"Yes, you are," her daughter told her. "You're not getting any younger."

"Nor's he." The Widow O'Hara pointed a gnarled and quivering finger at Inspector Rosher. "Why aren't you putting him to bed?" She gnashed her tooth at him.

Mavourneen addressed the two policemen. "Go on in. I'll be down in a minute." She piloted her mother firmly toward the stairs.

It wasn't bad, the lounge. The furniture was factory-spawned, by hire purchase out of the Co-op, but there was no peeling away of the bright paper, no damp patches on the walls. No smell of mice and unwashed clothing, no rotting window frames, no matted covey of scabby brats gazing bare-bummed and owlish with a finger in every mouth. No spread of odiferous nappies. If the flowers were plastic, what of that? They were given away at present with a new detergent. To amass a bunch, as here, was to give proof of clean intentions. The company would have been flogging a dead horse down this way, once.

The policemen stood around, for more than the promised minute. Four or five passed before Mavourneen came back. She said: "I've given her a Guinness. It helps her to sleep."

"Does she know about—er—the boy?" Inspector Rosher asked. Guinness in the old days started her battling.

"No. I'll tell her in the morning. I don't think I could cope with it tonight."

"Hmph," he said. "You understand I have to ask you some questions? And I'll need to see his room. His belongings."

"Yes," she said. "Would you care for a cup of tea?" Cop of tay, she pronounced it. Her mother would have called it a dish.

"No. No, thanks." The constable licked parched lips. It was the inspector who turned the offer down, without consultation. Typical. It's the poor who suffer. "When did you last see your nephew?"

"The day before yesterday."

"The day before yesterday?" Old Blubbergut was saying. "Not yesterday?" It seemed longer—it had been a long day—but the night of yesterday was when the fire blew up.

"No. No, I didn't see him yesterday."

"I thought you said he lived here."

"Yes. But he didn't come home the night before last."

"What about yesterday?"

"He didn't come home yesterday, either."

So he could have been dead two days. "Where did he go, do you know?"

"I never asked. He lived with me, that's all. I didn't run his life."

"Did he often go missing like that?"

"You know what they are, with their discos and their parties and their girlfriends."

"Had he got a girlfriend?" Girlfriends are often very useful, they know a lot that parents and guardians would be surprised to hear.

"He knows girls, I expect."

"Anybody special?"

"Brendan could tell you more about that."

"Brendan?"

"His friend, Brendan Mulcahy."

"Ah. Where can I get hold of him?"

"Well, I don't know. He works at Nore-Smiths, he's a checker. I don't know where he'll be now."

"What's his home address?"

"Ah. Well, now, you see—he's been staying here. Sharing Johnnie's room." Suddenly, she seemed uneasy.

"Uh-huh." Subletting, in a council property? Naughty. But he wasn't going to skop her. The constable might, but not a detective inspector. Too trivial. To his certain knowledge, everybody is working some sort of fiddle. You can't afford to spend mornings in court with all of 'em, you'd never get any real work done. Besides, they always have a get-out. Watch this. "Does he pay rent?"

"Oh no, no. I wouldn't have that. He's a guest only."

"How long?"

"He's been here three months. Just till he finds a place to lay his poor head."

This is how you always knew there was guilt about behind the limpid, child-innocent eyes: a deepening of the brogue, a conjuring up of the sentimental picture directed instinctively to the winning of sympathy. It was me sainted wife lying pregnant wit not a speck of food in te house made me punch the poor man in te pub, yer honor. "Rrmph," said Inspector Rosher. "I'll just have a look at the room."

There are three bedrooms in these houses. One, presumably—a bigger one, she'd need the space—would serve for Mavourneen. One, presumably—probably the little one—contained the old lady. In the other was a single bed, with a camp bed made up across the foot of it. Catholic boys do not share beds, because of the potential for sin. There was a closet with clothes in it, some of them belonging to this checker friend and the rest to the dead youth. Rosher took the latter with him, having dug through all the pockets and found nothing. They might, just might, yield something to the cunning manipulation of Forensic. What Forensic really likes a go at is the clothing subject was wearing at time of death. But in this case, of course, it was all burned up.

"Did your nephew have a job?" he asked, as they came back down the stairs. In a time of high unemployment it is by no means certain. With O'Haras, it never was.

"He had, but he was made redundant. Two weeks ago."

"Where was that?"

"He worked for Nore-Smiths, too. He was there before Brendan. Funny. Now he's out, and Brendan's still working."

"I thought the rule was last in, first out?"

"Different departments," she said. "And Johnnie is—was—more or less casual. Loading and unloading, washing down the trucks. Things like that."

She saw them off at the door. There were many questions he could have asked. What other friends the lad had, where did they live—all the routine by-the-book things, but this was not the time, while she was so clearly shattered by the boy's death. Not that the forebearance was rooted too deeply in sympathy; although in fact he did feel some, if only as by-product of sentimental nostalgia. But the press would be onto this one, and the press loves to bang the police. Given a defenseless widow-woman and—oh, joy—an old, old, old-age pensioner grandma, heartbroken and chivvied by a bull-bollocked copper in the moment of maximum grief—oh, frabjous day! Wise in his self-preservation, the inspector walked away. Nothing lost, really. He'd be back.

Down at the canal basin he found Superintendent Fisk with the Chief Constable. The area in front of the warehouse had been roped off by now, but there was nothing for anybody to do, on either side of the ropes, until the fire brigade organized the clearing of all that fallen rubble which, presumably, they were doing now. Nobody really believed there'd be much to see when it was all dug out. The work itself, necessitating many boots tramping about, all unable to avoid any specific area even if they knew where to avoid, would destroy what very, very little in the way of useful material might have been spared by the fire itself. But the police must not assume that nothing is there. At all times, follow the book.

When Rosher had made a brief verbal report, the Chief Constable said: "Good work, Mr. Rosher." It wasn't, particularly. A routine task, routinely carried out. But the good man was a firm believer in encouraging the troops. We all have our funny little ways. "I was just saying to Mr. Fisk, there doesn't seem to be much point in everybody hanging around here, it will be morning before the rubble is cleared. I suggest we leave a few uniform men to keep an eye on things, and a sergeant—Sergeant Roughage is around somewhere . . ."

"With the house-to-house, sir," said Fisk. House-to-house teams were working already.

"Good. Splendid. Reliable man. Let's have him back, shall we? Then I suggest you both go home. Get a few hours sleep. We know where to find you, if we need you."

Sound commonsense, really. No point in all the important brains standing about all night, wearing down while they watched a pile of rubbish diminish. This was a hiatus. Sensible detectives take advantage of any such lull at the start of a major inquiry, knowing that once the case breaks, they may go for days on end with no more proper sleep and a diet of sandwiches. The uniform man works shifts-and-overtime, so he does all right. The CID man grinds on until the job is finished. Or he is. Whichever comes first.

So when Sergeant Roughage appeared, he was given a terse and quite unnecessary briefing (he was a good man, turned forty and so less scrofulous than many), and the top brass, the second top brass, and Inspector Rosher turned away. The Ring o' Roses was closing now. From it were emerging half a dozen of the devout who linger in love, and Bert Humsey with Sydney, his driver, who said sotto voce: "There's dozens of the bastards."

"No there ain't," said Bert, as softly. "There's not more than half a dozen."

With sudden boldness, the driver said: "Ah, fuck 'em, anyway." He'd several large brandies taken. As they turned and went with the other drinkers toward the street that leads from the pub to the council estates, the Chief Constable was saying: "Did you bring your car, Mr. Rosher?"

"No, sir," said Rosher. "Left it at the station." No skin lost for this. He came down with Fisk.

"Splendid. I'll run you up for it. No need for you to bother, Mr. Fisk. You go home."

A few minutes, and the area was left to the moon, the firemen, and the policemen who needed to be here awaiting the rubble-clearing team. The house-to-house men were being called in for the night, because you cannot knock on people's doors once they are in their nighties. In the Ring o' Roses, Mr. and Mrs. Chafers were washing glasses, emptying ashtrays, doing the things Mavourneen usually did; not talking because they detested each other so. The narrowboats, the little cruisers sat quietly on the still water, and the truck squatted massive in the too small street between the warehouses. Nobody came near it.

When Superintendent Fisk reached home, he went straight to the drinks cabinet without even removing his hat. There was nobody else in the house; he knew it as soon as he opened the front door. It had been a strain, standing so long so close to the Ring o'

Roses, longing for a drink which he had not been able to call in for with the Chief Constable present and himself on duty. Not a drop had passed his lips since lunchtime.

Now he took half a tumbler of whisky at a gulp, sighed deeply with relief as warmth spread from the belly, quietening the quivering of his muscles, and filled the glass again. A long pull, to savor the bite, then he looked around.

It was a mess in here. She seemed not to be able even to open and adjust curtains properly; one side was pulled right back, the other sagged oddly as it never did in his first wife's day, halfway to closed across the pane. The windows looked dirty, the place had a musty, dusty feel. Her slippers lay beside an armchair just where she'd kicked them off, and on the arm of the chair stood a bottle of nail varnish, abandoned it open beside an ashtray in which a cigarette had been left to burn into a long column of gray ash ending in a lipstick-stained filter tip. And she'd gone out, as usual. Dancing. Or to the club where she used to work. He'd find a note in the kitchen.

He emptied and refilled his glass; went with it into the kitchen. There was the note, propped against a sauce bottle on the table. "Dinner in oven. Light gas. You weren't home, so I went out."

He thought: I don't think I'll bother, I can always make a sandwich. Or I could go out for a meal, the Chinese won't be closed yet. What I do think I could do with is another drink. I can't go out, anyway—can't leave the phone. Bed is what I chiefly need, but I doubt if the bed's made. If it is, it will only have been pulled together. I'll wait up. If she's gone dancing, she should be home soon after midnight. There's a fair dollop of whisky left in the bottle.

He'd always been a drinking man, Superintendent Fisk, but until quite recently, a jovial, social one. He drank in company then, a waggish and popular man—except with little villains, and some of them liked him—who happened to enjoy it. A very good policeman indeed, he had taken care to see that it never affected his work. Absorbed in a case, he often went for weeks without touching the stuff.

But then his two sons were killed. A motorbike, moving too fast into a country road bend, the driving son nineteen years old, the pillion rider sixteen. His wife sank then from comely and smilingly plump to thinner, to thin, to skinny, with great dying eyes ringed in purple and all the live, comfortable chatter replaced with silence broken by a sudden, jagged sighing. Six months later she died, leaving him all alone in this good house with only a ticking of clocks and the sudden neurotic, nerve-shredding eruption of the telephone where used to be noise and laughter and hi-fi and quarrels and a constant confusion of things the boys had scattered, and peace together, he and his wife, with supper and the television when he was off duty and they were gone out.

This was when he really began to hit the bottle. And thrown off balance by his state of increasing distress, he made the great mistake. In a condition almost of unsound mind, he married again.

She was not a brassy blond barmaid, nothing like that. But she did work part time behind the bar of a drinking club, operating well within the law, where he took to spending most of his leisure time. Acted as hostess, really. Very popular, gay in the good sense, ready with quip and laughter. A good listener to customers with troubles. Not that he spread his around. Too much pride, and they went too deep. Thirty-four, approximately, she was, and divorced. Attractive, warm, sympathetic, charming. No other details matter. He married her. Or she married him. A detective chief superintendent of fifty with his own good house and no encumbrances is a rare fish to come upon swimming loose.

It was all a public facade, of course, the uplifting gaity, the quick, warm sympathy. She was, he found, a slut in the house, given to sitting around all day among the unmade beds and the undone dishes reading cheap romances, smoking, and painting (she always seemed to be doing it) her toenails. The charm was used still, to ingratiate herself with the neighbors; but she no longer bothered to waste it upon him. And because his work kept him away often through the evenings—no CID man can afford to ignore the evenings, when the little men gather in pubs and clubs, grasses can be induced to whisper into a bought glass, and many crimes happen then, many arrests are made—she said she was bored (a common complaint among CID wives), and took to going out. Dancing, or visiting her old club, drinking now on this side of the bar.

He didn't blame her, he blamed himself. He should have known. There were pointers enough that he, an experienced policeman with professional interest in elementary psychology and knowledge of many women, should have snapped up. He had, he saw now, tried to use her, to comfort him in his distress. But she, it seemed, had used him. Hard luck, mate.

As the relationship deteriorated, so his grief and guilt mounted. Guilt, not toward her, but to his true wife, whom he had loved and still loved, whose cherished home and loved husband he had delivered over to a slut. And toward his sons, his proudly loved sons; because it was he who had bought the motorbike, capitulating to long pleading. You cannot, he'd told his objecting wife, featherbed them all their lives.

No, he did not blame his dancing barmaid. When it became clear that she was not, as he had believed, going to help rebuild his shattered life; when he saw that what he had here was not a supporting helpmate but the added burden of a weak and shallow lady with near-neuroses of her own, he drew the cork from the bottle again.

They knew about this, at the station. Not the riveting details, but the overall pattern of disaster. And policemen, probably because they live in isolation from the commonality by very virtue of their function, are a more than normally clannish lot. They fight each other, they quarrel, they scramble for promotion, they bitch about the man who beats them to it and the stupid bastards up there who elevated him. But under all this there is respect, liking, even love, especially between those who have faced the guns together, and when trouble comes to one proven and highly popular, as Fisk was, they close ranks around him. They support him, they hold the poor sod within a muscular and hairy arm. And he will be the last to know they are doing it, or if he survives to a steady afterwards, that they ever did it. The armed forces, the fire brigade, apply the same unspoken code.

So nobody looked from the side of the eye at Superintendent

Fisk, nobody made little snide jokes from behind the hand, as they did when Inspector Rosher, the gorilla-headed, elephant-hided, bombastic Old Blubbergut, came crashing down among them to a sergeant's desk, having grabbed a handful of mammalia protruding like the caps of twenty-five-pounder shells from the ribcage of a publican's wife. Which grab only lasted a second, and wasn't all that good. But then, you see, Inspector Rosher was well on the leeward side of popular; while Superintendent Fisk blew about nicely well upwind, esteemed as much for his personal qualities as for his considerable professional skill.

Even the Chief Constable, who had his mild eye on more things than many of his subordinates would have believed, took his part in this general closing of ranks, because whereas in his good days the superintendent's bottle-bashing never affected his work, now it touched it—but very rarely. A day sick, a delayed start, hangover to be coped with, hair of the dog sought. Nothing much. The fierce and lion-headed but spindle-legged man who previously occupied this office, and who cared not a bugger for esprit de corps or any such sentimental claptrap (he it was who bust Rosher down) would have had the man in, tongue-roasted him rigid, and told him to get up or get out. But this humane new Old Man (he it was who reelevated Rosher) was of different and less hairy stuff. So he kept an eye on the situation and trusted that it would all come right in time.

The time was not tonight. Superintendent Fisk sat with his bottle until half past midnight. And then, when she came in with a slight gin-wobble, she sneered at him for a dull old bugger, past dancing and all the joys of youth, to stay with while she rinsed her hair. Bubble Blonde. Until he snapped back at her, and they ended the day with a row.

5

Bert Humsey, his driver Sydney Kelly, Brendan Mulcahy, and Mr. Chafers all spent an uncomfortable night. If Mr. Nore-Smith knew by now, on the Continent or wherever he was, what had happened here, he probably had not rested too happily, either. Superintendent Fisk, when he finally got to bed, passed out until 4 A.M. and awoke to find he'd left the light on. Liquor is a great obliterator, but over short distances only. The Chief Constable slept very well; and Detective Inspector Rosher lay like the snoring dead from three minutes after he hit the mattress. He awoke early, helped by the inscribed alarm clock given to him as reward for smashing a fellow policeman flat to the canvas in his boxing days, and got up. Seven o'clock.

By eight, on another bright morning lightly touched with September mist, he had washed, shaved his solid chin until it gave off the desirable blue sheen, breakfasted on a bacon sandwich washed down with two mugs of that black and bitter tea without which, for him, no meal was complete; had rinsed the crockery under the tap because he had learned the hard way that a man whose fat wife went home to Mother long ago does well to stay on top of the dishes; and was in his car en route for the canal basin.

There would be a conference later in the Chief Constable's office, as always every morning during the course of a major investigation, but not until ten o'clock. Time to peer around here first. It looks well, to arrive for the conference after two hours on the job. If Ernie Fisk was compos mentis, he'd probably do the same.

He was able this morning to drive all the way down onto the quay, the barrier having been removed. The fire engine or one like it was here still, its crew playing their hose onto the rubble cleared now into a stack on ground where the wall had vanished completely. Probably they were doing it to kill time rather than to drown out possibility of a fresh eruption. No sign of the clearing party. They'd have worked through the night and gone home.

Detective Sergeant Roughage, poor man, was still on duty. That's CID work for you. At least he had been able to sit in a squad car—more than one, no doubt, because the uniform men would have been relieved—with the crew for company. He came out from the back seat when he recognized the black hat of Old Blubbergut driving down; wearing his overcoat, donned, of course, because September small hours are brutal, and kept on to combat the chill of weariness. His eyes were tired, his goodly quota of chin as blue as the simian jaw of the man ducking the black hat out from his car come to rest close by, but bristling where that one shone. He said: "'Morning, Mr. Rosher." Not Alf, you'll notice.

"'Morning," said Rosher. "Still here?"

A tired detective, provided he has rank, when asked a silly question is entitled to show irritation. To any other inspector, the sergeant would undoubtedly have said with a deal of asperity, "No, I went home hours ago." But this was not any other inspector, this was Rosher. "Uh-huh," said Sergeant Roughage.

"Anything happened?"

"Nope. The lads finished the clearing half an hour ago. Forensic's coming down." With the photographer—with the Scenes of Crime men, and the rest. No need to list them, Rosher would know.

"Seen Mr. Fisk?"

"Nope."

Good. First on the job, it brings a tincture of smugness. And it looks very nice in the book. "Uh-huh," said Inspector Rosher. This is a sort of grunt, made through the nose without moving the lips. Very common, among policemen. "Let's have a look."

They walked to the edge of the warehouse area, where they stood and gazed for a few moments. The sergeant said: "Ask me, they're wasting their bloody time if they think they're going to get anything out of that." He didn't specify who they were, but his tone said plainly: All *I'm* going to get out of it is a night without sleep and tight lips from the wife.

No good talking, CID work and marriage don't mix. Detectives should, as part of their terms of service, submit to castration very young.

"Uh-huh," said Inspector Rosher. He turned away. "Better hang about here. I'm going to nose about a bit."

Sod you, too, the sergeant thought. Any other bugger would have said, You go home, I'll hold the fort until the clever boys get here. He made the grunt again. "Uh-huh." Look at him go. Like a performing monkey.

Inspector Rosher was making off along the wide entrance used by the trucks, into the haulage yard.

The firm was in action already. Not the office. The new building that made the conservationists spit showed no sign of life, and wouldn't until half past nine; but the truck left overnight in the narrow street between the warehouses had been brought in and was being unloaded by a trio of men, one of whom manhandled the tallish, oblong cartons to the tailboard, from where the other two carried them into the big, cavernous store–cum–servicing open-fronted shed. At a little distance stood roly-poly Bert Humsey, talking softly with the driver Sydney Kelly. He was saying: "Stop bloody panicking. We'll have to use the next-door warehouse."

"There's bloody fuzz all over the place," said Sydney.

"Will you bloody listen. I'll send you out empty. All you gotta do is get lost in the city somewhere. Ring in this evening, I'll tell you if they're still here. If they are, we don't do nothing, you come back in and I'll send you on a job tomorrow, open-ended so you get back in the evening or stay out, whatever seems best."

"I'll still be carrying the stuff."

"Who's gonna know? You're working as usual, you're just going in and out like the others. They gotta clear off in the end, ain't they, the pigs? Then we offload like we always do, but we put it in the other warehouse."

"What happened to Johnnie?"

"How do I know? Hush up, hush up—here comes one of 'em."

"I told you they would, didden I?" the driver said. "I told you they'd come nosing around."

Inspector Rosher approached, black-hatted, durable-suited, hinderpart stuck out in a way that made his big, hairy knuckles appear to dangle round the knees; a mode adopted long ago to hide it when he found the fat wife's compulsive and irresistible cookery had fastened a little potbelly on him. The belly went with the wife, shriveled by a diet of baked beans and whatever came out of cans in the days before he learned to fry a little for himself (and scrag-end flung in the pot, rapidly boiled with assorted vegetables, makes a cheap and nourishing stew). But the posture remained, without his being aware of it. Piloting his boxy-toed shoes over the concrete, he thought now as he neared the roly-poly Bert: Funny-looking little feller. He said, with a brief glimmer of brownstone teeth: "'Morning. You the foreman?"

"'Morning," said Bert. "Yeah. Bert Humsey."

"Uh-huh. Got in all right, then?" The black hat nodded toward the truck, nearly offloaded by now.

"Your bloke let us through, seven o'clock this morning."

"You were up and about early."

"Didn't go to bed. Slept in the cab." This had seemed best to Bert, when the pub turned out last night. He'd sent Sydney home and taken guard duty himself, because he knew he could be trusted not to blow anything if a bored copper came chatting. Told Sergeant Roughage he'd be doing it, pointed out that there was valuable stuff on board and he had to watch the insurance. He repeated it to Rosher now. "Valuable stuff on board, and we have to watch the insurance."

"What are you carrying, then?"

"Washing machines. On contract. Pick 'em up in Holland, offload here, the firm collects 'em in their own trucks."

"Holland, eh?" said Rosher. "Get about a bit, don't you?"

"*I* don't," the roly-poly man said. "I'm stuck here, up to me gearbox in oil. *They're* the ones who get about, the drivers. Buggers like him." He jerked a thumb at silent Sydney. "They're the ones what gets the gravy."

"Well," the inspector said, "at least you've got a canal. All you need's a pair of clogs." He glimmered his incisors again, because this was a pleasantry, and should be acknowledged as such in the interest of public relations. In which field, when charm was called for he had no peer. Of this he was utterly convinced. But enough is enough. He sheathed himself decently. "The lad who was found in the fire, this John O'Hara. They tell me he used to work for you."

"Yeah. Mmm. Casual, really. When I needed extra hands. We get rush loads sometimes, a bit too much for our lads. Or two or three in together, all got a delivery date guaranteed. We take on casuals. One day, two days. He used to do a day here, week there, couple of weeks sometimes."

"Easy to get 'em, I suppose, all this unemployment about?"

"You'd be surprised." Bert's eyes were on the unloading gang. "Half of 'em don't want to bloody work, they do better on the dole. And then there's the unions." He wished Sydney would piss off, say he had to go to the bog or something. He was all stiff and glowering with nerves. You could feel it from here.

"Did he have any special mates?"

"Mates?"

"Anybody he used to knock around with?"

"No. Not from here. He only came in casual."

"I understand he had one of your staff lodging with him. A Brendan Mulcahy, been here about two months. In the office."

"Don't know nothing about that." Bert's heart was leaping. He added scathingly: "Bloody *office*. I dunno nothing about the office, I got enough to do keeping the bloody trucks running."

Blue-collar worker, white-collar worker—and never the twain shall meet. "How many you got?" the inspector asked.

"Five. And the fifteen-hundred weights, couple of vans."

"Lot of work for one man."

"You can say that again." Let's get off this, for Christ's sake. How can I tell you without starting you rooting that I fixed it that way? No nosy help needed. "It's all right, long as you keep 'em on the top line."

"What time's the office open?"

"Half nine. Jammy buggers. And they bugger off again at half five."

"Uh-huh." Two fifteen-hundredweight trucks, two light vans stood across the way. The only truck here was the one being off-loaded. "What happened to your other big stuff?"

"They all stayed out, your blokes wouldn't let me get 'em in. Some was on long runs, overnight. Figgers let me use their yard for the others, they'll be coming in any time." Figgers was another haulage firm, a mile or so away.

"Well, nice to talk to you," said Inspector Rosher. "If you think of anything to do with young O'Hara, let me know. If I'm not around, ring the station. Ask for Inspector Rosher."

"Right." One of the unloading trio was signaling, a thumbs-up meaning job completed. Bert addressed the driver. "All right, Sydney. Let's get you on your way."

The group broke, Rosher heading back to the quay, the others moving toward the truck and the cartoned washing machines stacked neatly now on the concrete platform of the bay. Sydney said: "Rosher. I seen him on the telly. He copped that Avenger. And them forgery geezers at Hutton Fellows. And them London geezers at the hospital."

"Never mind him," said Bert. "All you gotta do is make for the city, get in the big lorry park near the city center. You can stay there all day."

"What about if somebody takes the number?" Sheer nerves speaking.

"Don't be a twat, who's taking the bloody number?"

"The mileage'll show, won't it? On the tachometer."

"For Christ's sake—I'll fiddle the tachometer, won't I? You just concentrate on getting there without hitting anything."

Men had arrived on the quay while Rosher was away. Not a few of them, come in cars parked now along by the canal. He saw that activity now was concentrated around the burned warehouse, because these were the specialists who would have been finished with field work last night, had the wall not collapsed. He moved over to greet them briefly and moved away again. Nothing here for him to do; if he were needed, they'd call him. Sergeant Roughage was gone, relieved at last by a Sergeant Makepiece, to whom the inspector said: "I'm going round to Fifteen, Jubilee Street. Just round the back. That's where I'll be if you need me.''

''Hokeydoke,'' the sergeant said. An archaic expression, picked up from late night movies.

This idea of turning the moribund canal basin into a leisure complex with boats for hire and so on: it's a wonder somebody didn't think of it years ago. Given the glorious country through which the canal meanders and the surprising views of the city when it passes through, to say nothing of the unusual perspective of the town itself if you go the other way, pinching the nostrils as you pass the sewage works, it has to be a genuine amenity and probably a lucrative tourist attraction. Other towns with far less to offer have been doing it for a decade.

But Rosher was not thinking on these things as he walked along toward the Ring o' Roses. His eye had fallen upon the brightly painted narrowboats, three of them tied up side by side; and upon a stoop-shouldered man in a yachting cap working with mop and bucket on the narrow side deck of the inboard one, who after one glance turned his back as if he hoped not to be noticed.

Rosher knew that man, back view, side view, front view. He said when he came up, in the avuncularly jovial tone favored by your working policeman when he addresses the familiar little bent: ''Hello, Knocker. What are you doing in that hat? Running away to sea?''

The man started quite artistically, turning his capped head so that his eyes found Rosher over his shoulder. Across his cadaverous face spread the smile of pure joy in the meeting with which your little bent normally responds to that avuncular joviality. ''Well, Mr. Rosher. Fancy seeing you. What brings you down here?''

Knocker Davis, this was. Take your pick from three schools of thought as to how he got the name. One: that he would knock off anything not screwed down. Two: that when he did, invariably he was knocked off himself soon after. Three: that he looked like a door knocker. Strong resemblance to Marley's Ghost. ''Matter of murder, my son,'' said Rosher, never mind that the Knocker was older than he was.

The smile modulated to a mournful drooping. ''Ah, yeah. Terrible, ayn it? Nephew of her what works in the boozer, I believe."

"What are you doing here?"

"Working, Mr. Rosher, ayn I? I work here." He indicated the narrowboats. "Keep 'em nice and tidy. Dirty lot, some of them as hires 'em, you wooden believe."

"You mean somebody trusts you without nailing the boat down? Taking a chance, isn't he?"

The beam spread wider over the door-knocker face. His teeth were browner than Rosher's. Oh, much browner. You could compare them quite easily, as the inspector bared his in a smile that blended, without seeming difficulty, gorilla with wolf. "You will have your little joke, Mr. Rosher," the Knocker said. "Always was a proper caution, you was."

"How long you been doing this?"

"Since June, Mr. Rosher. When the season started."

"Bit of a change for you, isn't it, honest toil?"

The smile spread wider yet, right up to the jug-handle ears. "That's all over, Mr. Rosher. I'm on the straight now. Give me a chance, see, the boss did. Nobody never give me a chance before." Certainly not you, you old bastard.

"Who's he, then? Who's the boss?"

"Mr. Chafers. He owns the boats."

"He must have a beautiful nature," said Rosher. "When'd you come out of the nick?"

"May. Just before I started here. Very good about it, Mr. Chafers was."

"Well, don't go half-inching that bucket, you'll find yourself back in again."

"Not me, Mr. Rosher, I done my share of porridge."

He'd done that, all right. Cost the ratepayer a thousand times what he'd ever whipped, though you lumped it together and flogged it at auction. "Glad to hear it. Well, keep your hand on your halfpenny. Don't know anything about this lad, O'Hara, do you?"

"No. Only somebody done him, that's all I heard."

"If you cop anything, let me know. I'll see it gets to the beak, next time you're up." You never know, the old bugger might come up with something. He'd done a little whispering, in the past.

"You don't half like your little joke, Mr. Rosher," the Knocker said. "Always was a lad, you was. Hee hee hee. Well, I better get on."

He dipped his mop in the bucket. Sloshed water onto the narrowboat's immaculate topsides, yellow and red with the modern simulation of traditional castle-and-roses canal-boat decoration. Rosher turned away; turned back as a jest occurred to him, a genuine coper-bound quip. "See you, Knocker, next time you get a tug."

"Hee hee hee hee," said the Knocker, an agreeable audience if ever there was one. "Hee hee hee, Mr. Rosher." Getting a tug is cognoscenti talk for having the collar felt.

Witty, that, Rosher thought, as he walked through a sunny morning losing its early crispness, to Jubilee Street.

A smell of frying bacon wafted out from Mavourneen's house when she opened the door, apron around her ample waist and slippers on her feet. She gestured invitingly with a spatula as she stood back to allow him to pass that formidable bosom without unduly crushing it, and said: "Come in, Mr. Rosher. Go into the lounge, I'm just getting a bite of breakfast."

The lounge looked no worse than it had last night. Nobody had come to take the television back or to abstract the three-piece suite. It all looked rather nice, with the morning sun shining through lacy curtains. Smelled nice, too. There was the bacon about, with a dash of sausage and what was possibly kidneys. Such a bosom can be maintained only by constant effort.

Hardly was the inspector inside the room than the Widow O'Hara appeared, shuffling down, presumably from her bedroom, and in through the left-open door. She, too, wore slippers—men's slippers, a deal too big—and the hem of a nightgown showed beneath an aged but still serviceable dressing gown clutched round her withered middle. Her sparse hair was bound into metal curlers, and obviously she had hurried—the ancient are as curious as children—to see who was this she heard arriving. Presumably she had not known it was Rosher, because she said on a cackle of happy surprise: "Holy Mary, 'tis himself! Have ye come to pinch us, den?"

"Not today, Ma," he said, and glimmered the teeth at her.

"Ma, is it, and me old enough to be his own daughter? If Oi'd knowed it was yourself, Oi'd have made meself beautiful. What was te feller's name, him wit te truncheon?"

"Dancey. Barney Dancey."

"Och, and many's the dance Oi had wit him in me younger days. Dead now, Oi expect, God rest his soul." She cackled happily.

Either she still hasn't been told about the grandson, the inspector thought, or she didn't take it in. Poor old Nellie, what a way to end up. He thrust away the thought—one he had often now, without needing face-to-face confrontation with old age to focus it—It's not going to be all that long before it happens to me.

"Do ye have te arthritis in you?" the old lady was asking.

"No."

"Terrible it is, in te mornings. All across me back, and me feet's a trial to me. Dere's toimes whin Oi can hardly lift me glass."

Mavourneen appeared, without her spatula. She said: "Your breakfast's on the table, Mother. Will you come now and get it while it's hot?"

The Widow O'Hara's chin jutted. Chumbling around her tooth, she said: "Oi'm staying here. Oi want to talk wit te man."

Mavourneen spoke firmly. "Breakfast. You know how you hate it when your kidneys are cold." And she bundled the old lady out toward where the kitchen would be, shooing her along as though she were a chicken. The widow went grumbling. Once, it would have taken strong men with corded arms to get her to go at all. And that's old age.

When the big lady came back, she said: "Sorry about that. She's not what she was. She hates a cold breakfast. Would you care for a cup of tea, now?" The Irish are even more lavish in pressing tea upon you than are the English. So are the Portuguese, but the Portuguese do not come into the matter.

"No, thanks," the inspector said. "Does she know about—er—your nephew?"

"We haven't told her yet. We thought we'd let her get a good night's sleep in first." We would be the collective family. They'd have gathered for a family meeting. They'd be holding a wake, most likely. The need to be doing so was probably in Mavourneen's mind now, when she said: "Will we be able to—do you know when we can—have him home?"

I doubt if you'll want him when you see him, Rosher thought. He's not going to look pretty, laid out in a coffin. "That's up to the coroner," he said. "You'll be notified, of course. I just dropped in to see if you'd thought of anything. Might be of interest."

Now this was undoubtedly true. In view of his visit last night, he had suggested to the directing Fisk before he went home that there was not much point in the house-to-house teams calling while the home was in initial shock, since he and/or Rosher would be back there anyway. Too many police calls at a time of grief, too much pressure confuses people. Even leads to violent antagonism, if the people are from volatile stock and given to brushes with the law. So Fisk, seeing the truth of it, spoke with Rolli Rawlins, who removed the address from his list.

But there are varying levels of truth, and here is a deeper level.

Murder comes rarely to a smallish-town police force, and he who is instrumental in clearing a case wins kudos. Never believe that policemen are above the love of kudos. Young ones need them, to get a foot on the promotion ladder. Promoted ones need them, for further promotion. Old ones need them for self-reassurance, as the younger nibble at their heels. They have to show they can still do it.

This is how it was with Rosher. Soon, he must retire. The fact haunted him; the thought of suddenly being nobody at all, living on through inevitable deterioration, sapped his self-confidence. One more clutch of kudos, then. If he must go, let them at least know that he was still Old Blubbergut. Let him leave with blue chin high, a fresh scalp added to many fine ones already dangling from his belt.

This house was where the kudos trail began. This was there the necessary information was most likely to stem from. He had intended anyway to come back alone—Ernie Fisk was manipulatable these days, it would not be difficult. And Ernie Fisk had not turned up yet. So here was Rosher, all alone as he liked to be, asking his questions.

"No," said Mavourneen. "I haven't been able to think of a thing. Why would anybody. . . ? He had no enemies."

The routine questions all produced negative answers, which did not worry the inspector at all. They commonly do; but they implant themselves in heads and often some beautiful leads come later, after you have set minds in motion thinking along the right lines.

He would go away now. He'd just make sure that she *was* on the right lines, that she had it implanted in her that if anything did bob up in her she should bring it to him, personally. Probably she would anyway—he was the man she knew from childhood, he was the one who called. But make sure. "Well," he said, "I won't bother you further for now. If anything occurs to you, anything at all, let me know. I'll be around. If I'm not, ring the station. Ask for me."

"I will," she said. "I'll do that."

"Anything out of the ordinary at the pub," he said. "Or anywhere. Let me know about it."

"The pub?"

It is an accepted cliché, and it actually happens very often, that the guilty return to the scene of the crime. It had come to Rosher, as it would to any competent policeman, that if the present guilty felt this urge, and if he were local, he would be sorely tempted by the Ring o' Roses where either from the seating outside or through the bar window he could keep an eye on what was going on, with nobody wondering what he was doing there. He said: "Handy places, pubs, when they let you see what's happening."

"Yes," said Mavourneen. "Oh, yes. I hadn't thought of that."

He was doing now the thing that set experienced souls stumbling over their feet, trying to get out of the neighborhood. He was bringing out his great gray handkerchief. "The lad Mulcahy," he said. "Is he in?"

"Left for work early." She was just standing there, the great big innocent. "They lost the day yesterday; there'll be all the loads coming in, all the lorries to get out again. Left just before you arrived."

"I didn't see him."

"He'll have gone the other way, through the alley. It comes out at the back of the office."

"Uh-huh," said Rosher, and he blew his nose.

She went back, a full pace of thirty inches that caught her fatted calf against the settee so that she sat down on it with a plump, one hand flying to that solid superfluity of bosom. Eyebrows shot up over startled Irish eyes—long black lashes, handsome, really. She said: "Mother of Jesus!" It must have been a good settee, it hardly even bent.

"Wassat?" said Rosher, mopping up.

A second of echo-dying silence. Then came a hammering upon an out-of-sight door, a cracked and scarified voice crying to Heaven: "Pwhat is it, pwhat is it? Let me out! 'Tis tunder, 'tis a great bliddy tunder-storm, we'll all be struck in our beds! Holy Mary Mother of God—let me out, ye little bugger. Be wit us sinners now and—we'll all be struck—in te hour of our death. . . ."

Mavourneen yelled suddenly: "Shut up, Mother. 'Tis only the man has been blowing his nose. Get on with your kidneys."

"'Tis an almighty tunder-storm. Let me out, ye little bugger—"

"SHUT UP, MOTHER!" Mavourneen screeched, but the old cracked cacophony went on. She addressed Rosher. "Terrified of the thunderstorms, she is. Pay no heed, she'll crawl under the table in a minute."

"What do you do, then," he said, "lock her in?"

"I have to when there's somebody calls or she'd never eat her breakfast. Keeps running in and out all the time."

He could remember when it had posed problems, big strong men trying to lock her in the black wagon. "Uh-huh," he said. "Well, I'll be on my way."

Superintendent Fisk still had not arrived when he got back to the quay. The pub landlord was here, bringing empty casks up through the cellar flap, and Knocker Davis was working faithfully—that's how it looked from here—on the boats. The specialist men were still poking about, and a few rubbernecks stood on the bridge. Inspector Rosher checked his watch. Nine-fifteen. He set off for the haulage-firm office, where a smart girl with a body that would have stiffened him up no end, in the days before trauma stemming from the publican's wife tamed his libido at last, told him Mr. Mulcahy was in the loading bay, busily engaged in checking.

Sure enough, he found a young man in the loading bay, armed with a clipboard and a checking pencil. A thin, shock-haired young man dressed in the ubiquitous jeans and bomber jacket. The original truck was gone, another had taken its place, and the unloading gang was stacking its cargo alongside the stacked washing machines. Two more trucks stood along the entrance alley, awaiting their turns to come in. A busy day indeed. The inspector said: "'Morning. Mr. Malachy?"

"Mulcahy," the young man said.

"Ah. Brendan Mulcahy?"

"That's right." The youth's eyes did not come up from his clipboard.

"Detective Inspector Rosher."

"Uh-hnn."

"I understand you have been lodging with Mr. John Patrick O'Hara."

"That's right." Now the eyes came up, looking not at Rosher but at the work being done.

No need to mention that John Patrick O'Hara was dead. The lad would know, everybody knew. "I wonder if you can help me."

"Uh-hnn. That the lot, Jerry?" Yet another pleasant Irish accent, directed at one of the laboring trio.

"That's the lot," the man said.

"Take it away, Tom." The youth lifted the nice voice, to reach the driver high up in his cab. The engine started, the truck moved forward, angling across the yard so that it could back, and turn, and go its way past the waiting vehicles; one of which began to creep forward to take its turn in the bay.

"Mr. O'Hara. Did you know him well?"

"Well enough. Not all that well."

"You were sharing his room. Two months, I believe?"

"That's right."

"How did that happen?"

"I needed somewhere to live. When I first came. He said his auntie might put me up."

"Bit cramped?"

"I wanted to be near the job. There's no rooms around this way. The nearest is Summit Road, and they're crummy bedsitters. Cook for yourself on a gas ring."

Made sense. Summit Road was a fair distance away, and as Rosher knew well, self-catering is a terrible chore. If he was a penny-pinching young man, and he had the look, economy would come into it, too. Mavourneen, who should not be charging him at all, would not be caning him for too much. And presumably she fed him. He could even go home for lunch. Better than a pork pie in the pub, or self-wrought sandwiches consumed in the office. And a man may sleep merrily on a camp bed, if at the end of each week he can sit on it to count the pennies it is saving him. Cheese-paring was an activity the inspector could understand, and in the inner heart approve. A man of notorious frugality, he had been doing it all his life. He said: "Do you know if Mr. O'Hara had any special interests? Any particular friends?"

"We didn't live in each other's pockets. I believe he used to go dancing a good bit. Discos. I don't go for that sort of thing."

"His aunt tells me he stayed out some nights. Do you know where he went?"

"Parties, probably. He used to go to parties."

"But you don't know where?"

"No. I don't go to parties." Again the nice voice lifted, pointed at the man who seemed to be in charge of the workers. "Put that lot the other end of the platform, Jerry, it's all for McIntyre and Hockaway." And to Rosher, as the departing truck paused at the yard exit, hinting that they get out of the way: "Better step back a bit if you don't want your feet run over. I really can't help you at all, I'm afraid. It's a bad time to be asking, I'm all behind."

"And upset a bit, I suppose," Rosher said, stepping to the side, "over Mr. O'Hara's death."

"Yes. Yes." The truck crept past. They were flat against the wall. Certainly this was not the ideal time and place to be conducting an interview. Better leave it, come back if necessary when things had quietened down a bit. Or call after working hours at Mavourneen's house, speak to the young man there without the distractions. "Right," said Rosher. "I'll let you get on with it. Thank you for your cooperation."

"Pleasure." The youth spoke with the pencil between his teeth, put there to free his hands while he eased the bulldog clip and brought a fresh sheet to the top of the pack on the clipboard.

Rosher turned away. Turned back. "Where were you before you came here?" he asked. "Ireland?"

The lad's eyes flickered sideways for a moment before they dropped again to supervise his hands. "Coventry. I was in Coventry."

"Uh-huh," said Inspector Rosher. "Good morning."

Chief Superintendent Fisk was here now, standing on the quayside and looking at the activity around the burned area where the warehouse used to be, in company with a fat man in a fine suit and a felt hat who might normally have been jolly but at the moment was not. A shimmering Rolls-Royce ruled nearby, keeping kingly distance from the hoi polloi cars. Rosher moved across and said: "'Morning, Mr. Nore-Smith. 'Morning, Mr. Fisk." And look at the bloody great dark circles under and the watery look of your eyes.

"'Morning, Mr. Rasher," the fat man said. He did look put out. "Bloody fine thing, isn't it? Turn me back, the bloody place burns down."

"Dry as tinder, these old buildings, sir," said Rosher. Some of the vowel-mangling cut-glass telephone manner had come upon him. Not that there was anything upper-crusty about the fat man, aside from his suit; but he did have a double-barrel name, and a Rolls-Royce, and a lifestyle that hooted of money. And as rich ex-mayor he carried remarkable clout, in every direction. Such men demand the best, and it should be given to them. And if they call you Rasher, be big about it. "I believe you own it?"

"Not much left to own, is there? And tuppence-halfpenny insurance."

Ernie Fisk put a word in. "Mr. Nore-Smith just got back."

"Holland," said the ex-mayor. "We do a lot of business over there. Went on to France. Touring, they couldn't get hold of me. Caught the early plane this morning, been up all bloody night. Niggled the wife, first bloody holiday in donkey's years. Left her out there, she'll be happier on her own. Understand one of my casuals was found in it?"

"John Patrick O'Hara, sir," Rosher said. "Yes. Murdered, we believe." The other man's remarks were obviously directed to him. People sense it, when the senior officer is not in complete control, being a teeny bit under the weather.

"Nasty, nasty. Can't say I call him to mind, they come and they go. But—nasty. Poor little bugger. Gives you fellers something to do, though, eh? Well, better go and see what cockups my lot've made since I left. If you need me, I'll be inside. When you want a cup of coffee, we've got a machine on the wall."

"Thank you, sir," said Rosher. "Good morning."

"Good morning, Mr. Rasher. See you on the telly again soon, I suppose, when you've cracked this one. Wonder they don't give you a contract, can't stand that Terry Wogan. 'Morning, Mr. Fisk."

Fisk started, quite visibly, called back from misty distances. "Good morning, sir," he said.

They watched the fat gentleman move away, across the forecourt and into the glass-and-concrete building bearing his name in golden letters across the frontage. His feet were splayed, but his shoes were beautifully polished and the trouser creases razor-sharp. Rosher's eyes moved on to the gleaming Rolls-Royce. "All right for some," he said. "You won't buy one of them out of your pension.'' Pensions loomed quite large in his thinking, these days.

Fisk was sadly hungover, tired and unhappy. He'd lain from pre-dawn, when he awoke from self-obliteration, brooding half-drunkenly until seven; then he dozed again. Nobody woke him up, no alarm clock buzzed because nobody thought last night to set it. He came from bed fast when his eyes opened and he focused and saw what time it was. The action sloshed his brains about in a skull that began enthusiastically to expand and contract with a familiar agonized pounding. He wobbled on his feet.

She'd stirred when he leaped from the bed, and opened one eye. Made the grunt that meant last night's quarrel was not over and turned her back, pulling the quilt high above her shoulders. Looking at her with his sick eyes, he wondered how the hell he came to marry her, how he had thought to fill with her the place in the bed, the house, his life, that belonged to his real wife.

She did not even get up to make him a cup of something. He brewed his own tea, and used it to wash down a hurried breakfast of aspirin. He took a hair of the dog. The sun smote his eyes cruelly as he drove down to the canal basin. It smote them still as he stood beside Inspector Rosher and made reply. A hurried go-round with the electric razor had left his chin slightly fuzzy, seen beside Rosher's scraped blue sheen.

''Nice. Not for the likes of you and me. What did he say about coffee?''

''They've got a machine. Wouldn't recommend it, personally.'' The gnat's-water that comes out of those machines won't do you any good, my son. Black, hot, and strong's what you need. Look at your hands, they're shaking.

''Mm. Well, I suppose we'd better get up to the Old Man's meeting. You've—er—been working?''

''Uh-huh.''

''Any joy?''

''Nothing.''

''Sorry I wasn't here. Got . . . tied up a little.''

''Uh-huh. No harm done.'' On the contrary. Happy start to the day, doing it my way with nobody breathing down my back. ''Whose car?''

"Mine. Leave yours here, we'll have to come back."

Hope you're fit to drive the bloody thing, thought Rosher. You still look half-cut to me. By rights, I should bar it; but I can't do that. Not without putting in an official squeaker. And you're the boss. Think of the ramifications. I've had enough of disciplinary enquiries.

But suppose you get knocked, me sitting beside you? Makes me an accessory. Sod that. Mistake to ask, wasn't it? He said: "I think I'd better take mine up. Keep it handy, in case I have to come back on my own." Which I could do in a squad car. But this is the best I can manage, off the cuff.

Fisk did not press the matter. It was Rosher's choice, really, where he chose to have his car. "Up to you," he said; and they walked away to their separate vehicles, parked in the line along the canal side of the quay. But with his hand on the door handle, he paused, said: "I think we'd better go up together."

Policemen like Rosher do not need every t crossed. They know, when it dawns on a man that he'd better have cognizance of the morning's activity before he leads his junior into an Old Man's meeting. He said: "I was thinking we've got time to stop for a cup of coffee on the way, sir. I'll need to fill you in on the details." It must have been the first time he ever awarded a sir to Ernie Fisk.

"Ah. Yes. All right," the superintendent said. "Blue Dahlia? We go right past it." He ducked his bothersomely whoozy head, and climbed into his car. Another policeman who did not need the t's crossed.

He didn't even get off the dock, poor man. Not unscathed. What happened was as follows.

Rosher, first man to arrive this morning, was parked well along the quay toward the Ring o' Roses end. Subsequent arrivals, all those specialists, had lined up behind him, except for Mr. Nore-Smith, who left his lovely Rolls on the landward side a car's length away from the rest, opposite to where Mr. Fisk, last to arrive of the policemen, had left his at the end of the line.

Now Mr. Fisk, when he came to drive away, needed to back a yard or two to clear the car in front of him, he having come a *leetle* too close to pull away without it. He could then drive straight on, quitting the basin by the road at the pub end, and threading through the council estates; or he could make a loose U-turn, going right round the Nore-Smith thoroughbred and on, to the slope by the bridge and the main road; or a very tight U-turn, to clear the Rolls on this side and voilà—up the slope and away. Three possible courses of action, none of them complicated. Plenty of room, no need to rush.

He chose the third, and the choice was bad. Any other morning, yes. Not this one. He backed all right, he came forward, twisting the wheel; but perhaps he missed a twist. He did not clear that Rolls. He bumped it, a glancing blow. Not a serious blow, but he bumped a Rolls. As well for a man that he goose the queen.

Rosher saw it happen. He was just approaching his own car. He thought: Oh, you silly sod, and plausible phrases sprang at once to his mind for use later, in case he had to assure the Chief Constable that no, sir, I saw nothing in Mr. Fisk's manner or appearance to suggest that he was not fully compos mentis and fit to propel a mechanical vehicle along the public highway. He turned, and began to walk back. The specialists had paused in their hopeless prying and were standing upright, rubbernecking to see what the twat had done. Not one of them but had his lust fixed upon that motorcar.

Mr. Fisk had stopped his car and was out of it by the time Mr. Rosher arrived. They looked at the damage. Not serious, if you consider it as happened to your common cooking-foil car; but this was a Rolls, and it had a scag and a dent low down on the rear door, where the end of the policeman's bumper took it. "Mm," said Rosher. "Uh-huh."

Mr. Nore-Smith came hurtling fatly out of his concrete building. It may be that somebody in there told him. It may be that the man who owns a Rolls develops sensitive antennae that keep him au fait with its condition at all times. Be that as it may, he came hurtling; and when he had bulged his eyes at the coachwork, he cried very loudly: "How the bloody hell did you manage that?"

"The um—the er—" said Mr. Fisk. But Mr. Nore-Smith was not waiting, he was hooting straight on.

"All the bloody room in the world and you hit the bloody thing!

I thought you was pissed when I was talking to you.'' He pointed a quivering finger and hooted at Rosher. ''He's pissed! You can prove it—he's pissed as a bloody nun.'' What a funny thing to say. Whoever saw a pissed nun? Few but the Mother Superior.

''Er-rrrgph,'' said Rosher.

''I demand a blood test!'' cried Mr. Nore-Smith. In just such a tone had he hollered for a recount, when they voted him off the council.

It is a relief to any policeman when the conversation veers and presents a way to avoid confirming that a superior rank is pissed, or arguing about it. Rosher nipped off very smartly. ''Breathalyzed, I expect you mean, sir.'' Blood testing is for horses. ''That calls for special equipment.''

Mr. Nore-Smith waved a fat arm. ''They're all police cars, ain't they? They must have it in the boot.''

''Those are all specialists' cars, sir, they don't do tests. And Mr. Fisk is senior rank here. I'm afraid only rank senior to himself is authorized to carry out such tests. *If* such a thing were necessitated.'' No vowel-mangling here. And all this time Ernie Fisk stood there, saying nothing. He spoke now, and somehow his authority was gone.

''I'll pay for the damage.''

''*Somebody*'ll pay for it,'' snapped the fat man. ''Do you know what it costs, bumping these things? The Chief Constable will hear about this. He's a personal friend of mine.''

More relief. The return to familiar ground always puts a certain comfort under the feet, and very few people frothing against the police are not personal friends of the Chief Constable. The rookie learns this with the first tramp he moves on, first day on the beat. So Rosher said, ''Very good, sir,'' and the fat man stormed away, back to his office without even exchanging insurance details.

They watched him go. Then Fisk murmured: ''Silly thing to do. Well, better be on our way.''

A minute or two later he drove off with Rosher following, under the tittering eye of all those specialist men with nothing better to do.

Mr. Chafers, of course, was among those present, manhandling metal casks out from his cellar in readiness for collection by the brewer's dray. His wife, drawn by the instinct that tells a beady woman that something is happening outside more interesting than what is happening indoors, had joined him. They watched Mr. Nore-Smith's arm-waving and pudgy departure back to his office. They watched the policemen's short conference and their driving away. Mr. Chafers said, addressing himself and the sunny air, "Bloody idiot."

"I've known you do some daft things in your time," snapped his lady wife. "What about Christmas, nearly backed us all into the bloody canal."

"Will you bloody well shut *up,*" said Mr. Chafers.

"I'll shut up, all right," his lady wife said. "One of these days I'll shut *you* up. For good. Mark my words."

"Sod off," he said.

Random shots in a war that went on daily, all day and every day. Had done for twenty years, ever since the shotgun wedding soon after which she miscarried, making the whole thing unnecessary, cake and all. "God knows why Edwin and Milly stay together," their relatives all said at bunfights and places where they gathered, "they'd be better off apart." Their friends would have said it, too, but they had no friends.

6

The Chief Constable's conference did not last long. There was not much to discuss. No obvious leads sticking up from the house-to-house reports; nothing positive from the specialist men, who had only just been able to move in and held out no hope anyway; nothing of fishy savor marking any part of Rosher's verbal report; nothing whatever from Chief Superintendent Fisk.

Waste of everybody's time, perhaps, but then again, perhaps not. Hiatus is common at the beginning of a major inquiry, and a

Chief Constable knows better than to postpone his setting up of a daily meeting because of it. Very often some chance thought from a policeman, displayed here, will spark in other minds the reaction that starts the hounds baying. Even when this does not happen, when you have men like Rosher it pays to emphasize every morning that in this force, we work as a team. And heck, what does it cost? A few cups of coffee and a packet of Cokernut Cream biscuits.

The chief himself broke the meeting up. After all, nobody else could do it. He said: "More coffee, anyone? No? Well, thank you, gentlemen. You will keep me in the picture, of course."

Of course. He'd be asking for trouble who didn't. The gentlemen turned to file out: Chief Superintendent Fisk, Chief Superintendent Rolli Rawlins, Detective Inspector Rosher, thankful again that the fiddling little bone china coffee cup had not come to pieces in his hands, and Detective Inspector Young Alec Cruse, who would oversee the team working here at the station, correlating bumph and verbals coming in from the field workers. No sergeants, none had been assigned as yet. The chief said, impassively: "Mr. Fisk, I wonder if you can spare me a minute?"

Mr. Fisk held back. The other men left. When the door had closed behind them, the chief picked up a paper from his in-tray and eyed it as he spoke.

"I've just had a telephone call from Mr. Nore-Smith."

"Uh-huh." The old bugger hadn't wasted any time.

"He says you have severely damaged his—er—Rolls-Royce."

"I wouldn't say severely, sir, no."

The chief put the paper down. "What happened, exactly?"

"I misjudged the distance. A tight turn."

He says you did not have to turn there, you could have gone straight on or round the back of the car. *He* says you were under the influence. "He appears to be very . . . upset . . . about it." Only the last was said aloud.

"So I gathered." Fisk had produced his pipe and baccy pouch. He was stuffing the one out of the other. Sweet-smelling flake he used.

The chief looked at him. He didn't seem half-cut. Seemed firm enough on his feet. But then, there had been times of late when the fume came from him in waves, and he stood without a wobble. His chin was a bit fuzzy, his eyes looked watery, but there were men here in this very station who rarely touched a drop and looked habitually worse. Chief Superintendent (Percy) Fillimore sprang to mind.

Fisk, of course, had sobered by now. The embarrassing episode jolted him toward it, the drive with the window down completed the job. He put his pipe into his mouth and looked firmly back into the chief's eyes. The chief said: "Well—mm. Unfortunate. He appears to have gathered the impression that you were . . ." half-cut, schickered, hard-pressed, a bit pissed ". . . that you had somewhat—overindulged."

"At that time in the morning, sir?" Nothing ruffled about Fisk. No dropping of eyes, no fumbling, no foot-scuffling. He simply stood foursquare and took the sensible line, lighting the pipe with a steady hand. It called for conscious effort.

"Mm. Yes. Bit—extreme." Or is it? Have you got to where you start at breakfast time? It won't cure your troubles. It's compounding them. As it is bound to do.

Look: This is a flea-bite, I shall bury it. If it were the current mayor, I might have to push it, but not now, when you are heading a murder inquiry. As it is, Nore-Smith is only ex-mayor, and voted off the council at that. Let us say he is right, and you were under the weather. He'd have to push to prove it. Rosher was there—but Rosher, surely, would stand on your side. No, apart from the embarrassing nuisance if he gets after me at the golf club, forget Nore-Smith.

But: are you fit to head a murder inquiry? Or are they overwhelming you, the troubles leading to the bottle, the bottle leading to bigger trouble? I've driven with you, you don't bang into Rolls-Royces belonging to men who still command clout. Perhaps I shouldn't have given it to you. But you were available, you were in line. To pass you over would have been a clear statement of—well—doubt. Mistrust.

"Very extreme, sir," Fisk was saying. He was even making a

joke. "Nobody's started that early since Errol Flynn." Not a good joke, nothing like that. But a joke, identifiable by the jocular tone.

"Yes. Yes." The chief twitched the corners of his lips a trifle, in acknowledgment. His thinking went on:

And half past nine is late to be starting work, on a murder case. Nore-Smith says you were arriving as he drove up. And only Rosher has put in a report. It seems he was there at eight. Perhaps I should take it away from you. But no, that would be public humiliation. Last straw it could be, on top of your other troubles. You're too good a man, privately and professionally, for that. And who else have I got? Percy Fillimore? He's tied up with the courts. Besides—Fillimore and Rosher? No. Oh no. We keep them well apart, don't we?

Rosher works well with you, you seem to have the right mix. It's a knack, working with Rosher, and I think you've got it. And Rosher, not mixed with Percy, is a good man, an experienced man, well able to prop you if you have to be propped. Take this Nore-Smith thing. Had Fillimore done it, Rosher would have shopped him like a shot. But it would take a shrewd operator to get him to agree that you were under, if you *were* under. Given that, I can hint that Nore-Smith should watch it, I can nudge him right away. And Rosher never so much as hinted that he worked alone from eight o'clock until you appeared at half past nine.

So far as Rosher can team with anyone, he can team with you. And that enhances *his* usefulness—and by God, he's a worker—where putting him with Fillimore nullifies them both.

Yes. So, I'll leave it with you. But don't do anything stupid, will you?

Thought moves so fast that there was no discernible pause between his acknowledgment of his subordinate's little jest and now, when he said:

"All right, Mr. Fisk. Thank you. I doubt if we shall hear any more about it, although I suppose you'll have to make good the damage. Knock-for-knock, eh? Probably best to settle it privately, keep your no-claims bonus. You'll be going back there now, I take it? Might be as well to call in, pour a little oil."

"I'll do that, sir," said Fisk.

"Good, splendid. Keep me in the picture." It sounded as though he meant in the matter of Nore-Smith. In fact, he did not. He always said it when his men girded their loins and set off to work. Almost a reflex habit.

At about the time when Superintendent Fisk left his chief's office, pausing on the carpeted landing to wipe palms gone coldly sweaty, Mavourneen Leery, née O'Hara, finally took her mother into the living room and broke the news of Johnnie's death. It had to be done sooner or later. Do it now, before the neighbors began to come calling, avid to express horror and sympathy and to find out what they could. The family would be back, too, although they'd probably leave it until she returned from work.

It took a little time and effort to tap through into the Widow O'Hara's aged skull. Completely self-absorbed, as is right and proper at her age, she was sulking and snarling still at having been denied the full benefit of Inspector Rosher's visit. Also for being lied to regarding the sudden clap of frightening thunder that never was nobody blowing his nose and may God forgive you for the fib.

When the fact registered, she lifted up her arms with gnarled little fists clenched freckled at the ends, and shook them with her face turned up to Heaven, crying in a surprisingly strong voice: "No! No! Not Johnnie! Te cow—she's lying to me again!"

"Mother, Mother," Mavourneen said gently. "Sit down now, sit down. I'll make you a cup of tea . . ."

"Tay? Tay? Tay, is it?" the old lady cried in that big, fierce voice. And then she collapsed into her chair, covered her face with her hands, and burst into keening tears. He'd always been her favorite, had Johnnie. Best beloved of all her children's children.

Also at this time, Bert Humsey sat in his little cubicle office down among the oily truck parts. He had a desk here, and a small, greasy-thumb–marked filing cabinet, and he had just been bringing the still-fuminous Mr. Nore-Smith up to date, outlining with the help of various greasy chits and dockets the situation as it had developed during his absence, particularly since the fire that licked up his warehouse. Doing a great job, Bert was, under very difficult circumstances. Even Nore-Smith, who had come in after rampaging through the office, had to acknowledge this, and so refrained from stamping on his foot.

He was just leaving when the telephone rang. Not the one that went through the switchboard but the other one, installed so that drivers who met trouble out in the big wide world could reach Bert with a minimum of fiddling about. All haulage businesses use some such system. Nore-Smith paused in the doorway, because it was his firm.

Bert picked up the phone and said hello. The phone said: "Is that you? What's happening? I've got into the lorry park—have I got to hang about all day?"

"Dallamires Lane," Bert said loudly. "You'll see their place halfway down." He looked at Mr. Nore-Smith, leaving the mouthpiece uncovered as he addressed him, in the hope that the caller would take the hint. "Syd Kelly. Can't find Hector and Gimble's, he's never done the run before."

"Bloody drivers," snorted Mr. Nore-Smith. "Couldn't find their arses, half of 'em." He stomped away. Bert spoke to the phone again.

"What the hell are you doing, ringing this time of day? I don't want to hear from you till five o'clock."

"Sod what you want—I'm hanging about here like a spare prick. I want to know what's going on, don't I? What's this about Dallamires Lane? Where's bloody Dallamires Lane?"

No bottle, that was Sydney's trouble. Fine when things were going right. A liability, it seemed, when snags appeared.

"Listen, you twat, the old man was in here. Wonder he didn't hear you. Now get off the line—and don't ring back till five o'clock." Slam. Down went the phone. Dallamires Lane, incidentally, is in Ripon. North Yorkshire. A long, long way from where Sydney was.

Outside in the sunny yard the trucks were coming and going. The firm's trucks, offloading what should have been here yesterday; the odd smaller vehicle come from various firms to collect and transport goods home. The loading gang had been augmented to six, and young Brendan Mulcahy was busy with his clipboard. No sign of the Chafers, man or wife, they long ago vanished into their pub, not far from which Knocker Davis, having briefed a couple of narrowboat hirers on how to engage forward and reverse gears and how to turn the craft, all during a five-minute run along the canal, told them where to get fuel when they needed it and waved them goodbye. One hundred and fifty pounds for a week of doing what the old boatmen drew pay for doing, every week of the year. How things have changed. Especially for the old boatmen, who are all dead by now.

Bert stepped out from his office and roly-polyed over to where young Mulcahy stood. He said, loud enough for all to hear if they cared to listen: ''All right, Brendan? I'm bringing Gary in next, want to get him away.'' And much softer, using the side of the mouth, ''If the Old Man mentions Sydney, he's gone to Ripon. Hector and Gimble's.''

Mulcahy operated the same technique. ''Ripon? Back tonight?''

''I know, I know—the twat rang in, the Old Man was there. I had to say something.'' Ripon and back—long trip, for one day.

''It'll have him over his hours. And the tachometer . . .''

''I can fiddle all that.'' And he'd need to, if Sydney came back tonight. As he must; he couldn't stay forever in the city park. Not with all that gear aboard. ''You just see he's gone to Ripon, if the old get says anything.'' Christ, I'd better make out a docket, too.

Mr. Fisk and Mr. Rosher held a short conference when the latter came down from the Chief Constable's office. If there was embarrassment in the senior man, he puffed on his pipe and did not let it show. And it took a great deal to embarrass Rosher. He knew, and he knew Fisk knew he knew, why the Old Man had requested that the superintendent spare him a minute. Fatso had been on the blower, belching about Ernie Fisk being Brahms-and-Liszt. Rosher had expected that he might be called into it, and he had set his mind to wary. But here was Ernie Fisk, and nothing seemed to be headed this way, so thank Christ for that and let's get on with it. And if Ernie Fisk was coming to pieces on the job, hard luck for Ernie Fisk. But if it meant that he, Rosher, was going to be leading the way, working to his own rules, well, it couldn't all be bad.

So they held this short conference and agreed that they had nothing much to get hold of. They went again through the house-to-house reports, and Rosher outlined once more his work of the morning, filling in more detail than he had given at the meeting upstairs. These things done, and a couple of calls taken from the press, who were told that the investigation was being vigorously pursued, Fisk said: "Well, cup of coffee, and I suggest we get back down there, see what the boys have dug up."

He needed that coffee. Not that any police canteen deals out a decent cup; but instant spooned from a big fat tin does at least moisten the parched lips and goes some way to combat boozer's dehydration.

They drove again down to the canal basin, each in his own car. The damaged Rolls stood there still, quite unabashed by the scag in its coachwork. The specialists were packing up, putting things into the trunks of their cars, putting themselves in, leaving only a constable to guard the roped-off area. Not much good fiddling about here, they said. They were taking earth samples, bits and pieces for analysis; but don't, they said, bank on anything coming from it. And one by one, they drove off.

While Fisk and Rosher were watching them go, Mavourneen came out from the Ring o' Roses to place the little chairs around the tables on the forecourt. Rosher said: "There's the lad's aunt. I'll just have a word with her."

"Right," said Fisk, and they walked toward the pub. When they got there, Rosher addressed her without taking off the black hat. This, because although she was undoubtedly a female member of the general public and so entitled, all other things being equal, all other things could not be seen as equal. She was an O'Hara, and no O'Hara woman had ever been entitled. Entitlement was for respectable female members of the general public. When was an O'Hara, regardless of sex, respectable? Also he knew her as a thumb-sucking kid in droopy drawers. These considerations kept the hairy hand from the brim. He spoke quite mildly, though.

"Good morning." He'd said that earlier, but it slipped out again. "Have you informed your mother yet?"

"Yes," said Mavourneen. "When she'd had her breakfast."

"How'd she take it?"

"Badly. She always liked Johnnie best. Her favorite, he was."

"Inside, is she?"

"No. No—she was carrying on. I've got Bridget in to look after her. There's a couple of bottles of Guinness in the larder."

"Uh-huh." Rosher addressed his superintendent. You have to include them in. "This—er—lady's mother is Mr. O'Hara's grandmother."

"Ah," said Fisk. "How do you do?" And he did raise his hat. "You are the boy's mother, then?"

"His aunt," said Mavourneen, looking a little surprised. "One of my brothers is his father."

"Ah," Fisk said again.

Still not with it, is he? Rosher thought. Aloud, he spoke to Mavourneen. "Well, don't forget what I said. Anything you think of, let me know." And now he lifted the hat, an inch above his short-back-and-sides. Any man who doffs in this day has to be knocking on a bit. It goes with pension books, and the beckoning finger of the undertaker.

The two solid policemen walked away. Mavourneen returned to her setting out of chairs and flicking at things with a duster. Fisk said: "Who else is around here we ought to have a word with?"

"Only the staff in Nore-Smith's office," Rosher told him. "And they leave every evening at five-thirty, doubt if they'll be much help. There's the souvenir and fancy goods, in the next warehouse."

Fisk was not ready yet, not ready at all, to face Nore-Smith again. "Let's have a look at the fancy goods," he said.

What once was the warehouse office had been very nicely tarted, the space increased by moving the back wall further back yet, into what had been the main storage area. The result was a long, brown-

and-white-paint–decorated shop, hung here and there with beige open-weave drapes, the color of Rosher's teeth. There were standard lamps set about, with big shades painted with canal themes, and on long covered tables a wide variety of miniature narrowboats; books and booklets dealing with canal history, canal cookery, canal locks, canal birds, the flora and fauna of canals, canal pubs, canal bridges, canal locks (second edition), and basket weaving; and home-produced marmalade, peach preserves, apricot jam, bilberry jams. There were calendars showing canal scenes and aprons with canal designs upon them. It could have been a jumble, but everything was laid out very neatly.

A tall man entered from a door in the back wall. Young, you'd have said; and then, nicely preserved, anyway. Under a mop of corn-colored hair his lips curved up in the eager smile of a curate's wife greeting the bishop for tea with fruitcake. His corduroy jeans were cerise, and he wore a flower-sprigged sleeveless waistcoat over a mauve silk shirt with what could have been a Peter Pan collar, and it wouldn't have surprised Rosher in the least.

He cried brightly—and oh, he had beautiful teeth—"Hel-*lo*. Didn't hear you come in, we can't seem to get the *bell* fixed. Were you wanting something?"

"'Morning," said Fisk. "Detective Chief Superintendent Fisk. This is Detective Inspector Rosher. We're from the police." He flashed the little leather wallet containing his ID card. Rosher didn't bother.

The tall man's mouth remodeled itself into a red-rimmed O, his eyes opened wide. "Not *the* Inspector Rosher?" he cried, flapping a long-fingered hand as if dealing a playful slap. "Not the one who was on the telly?"

"Uh-hmph," said Rosher. He was thinking: I know you. Were you ever nicked?

"Oh, but we *saw* you! We're absolute *fans.*" He lifted up his voice. "Peter!"

Out came a middle-sized man, and this one definitely was young. Not so young as to have to say No to a consenting adult, so long as he was asked in private, but not much older. He was slim and willowy—there is no other word for it—and his wavy hair glowed a rich, lustrous beechnut brown. He wore a white boutique boilersuit splashed with paint and he carried a paint-roller.

The first man cried: ''Peter, *who* do you think is *here?* Inspector *Rosher*—you know, we saw him on the *telly*. He looks just the same, doesn't he? A little bit taller, perhaps, but that's because he's so *broad*. It made him look shorter.''

''Oo,'' said the newcomer. ''Fancy!''

''This is my friend Peter,'' said the taller man.

''Hello,'' said Peter. His teeth were every bit as good as the other's, and his lashes were longer. He flapped them when he smiled.

''*Massive* shoulders,'' said the tall one; and perhaps to avoid hurting the feelings of Superintendent Fisk, ''So have you, but of course we've seen Mr. Rosher on the telly, we're *bound* to be a bit excited. I'm Clovis.''

''Clovis?'' said Fisk, as Rosher, seeing the pair together, was thinking: Last night. That's it. Drinking outside the pub.

''Clovis Henderson. Clovis as in Saki.'' Up went a trilling laugh. ''What can we do for you? Haven't done anything *naughty*, have we?''

''The fire next door?''

Both men stretched their eyes. ''Isn't it *terrible?''* said Clovis, giving the air another slap. ''Good job it didn't spread to here, they say it would have done if it hadn't been for the wynd.''

''The wind?'' Fisk said.

''The alley—the wynd—the little street in between. They *say* it's a miracle it didn't jump the gap. And we've only *just* got the place looking ticketty-pookins, we're still *painting*. Well, you can *see*.'' He indicated his friend, who held up the paint-roller.

''A young man died in it.''

The bright smiles dwindled. ''I *know,''* said Clovis. ''Isn't it *terrible?* Poor boy. *Awful*. But they say he was dead before the flames got at him. That's a mercy.''

''Did you know him?''

''Well, of course, we know *all* the firm's boys. To speak to, that is. Don't we, Peter?''

"Very good-looking," the youth said. "Lovely broad shoulders. Beautiful eyes, most of the Irish boys have."

Clovis lost his eager smile, turned suddenly waspish. "You don't have to make a meal of it, duckie."

"Do you know anything about him?" Fisk asked.

"We didn't *mix* with him," the older man said, bringing the smile back. "We only knew him to *speak* to. In passing, as it were. Though I don't doubt *some* of us would have liked to know him better."

"You've no idea how he came to be in the warehouse? Did any of the lads, the staff, use it for any reason?" Off-the-record boozing, because drivers in from the Continent might well invite general participation in the duty-free. Then there is glue-sniffing, very popular in old abandoned buildings. And pot-smoking, which calls for matches easily dropped by anybody who, on a trip gone wrong (not on pot, but there's hard stuff about, among soft-drug aficionados) has staved a fellow puffer's head in, for some or no reason. A small quarrel, a whim, or because the victim suddenly looked like a purple monkey or the devil in a bile green suit.

"*We* wouldn't know, would we? We're not *watching* them all day. At least, *some* of us aren't."

"What about after hours? Have you noticed anybody going in and out in the evenings?"

"We're not *here* in the evenings, are we? We're *gone* by five o'clock."

Rosher put a word in. "You were here yesterday evening. Drinking at the Ring o' Roses."

"Oh, well, *yesterday*. That was different, wasn't it? They wouldn't let us in here all day, we wanted to see what was going *on*. Naturally."

"Mm," said Fisk. "Well, thank you. If you do think of anything that might help us, we'll be grateful if you'll get in touch."

The smile was back in quantity. "Of *course* we will," Clovis cried, flapping that hand again and batting coyly at the inspector. "We'll ring the *station* and ask for Mr. Rosher."

The policemen turned to leave. Clovis moved with them, toward the door. "Nice little place you have here," the superintendent said. It pays to be sociable. People warm to you, they remember better if you massage their egos.

"It *will* be," Clovis said, "if we ever get it *finished.* So much *work,* we've got all the *basement* to clear and *everything*. Good job we know how to handle a brush. Although I'm not sure brown and white is *altogether* ticketty-poo for in here."

"Good morning," said Fisk. They were out in the sunshine now.

"Tatty-poo." Clovis beamed. He turned the beam to the inspector. "Bye-ee, Mr. Rosher. See you on the telly." And he waggled his fingers.

They moved away. Fisk said: "Well, well, well. You've made a hit." It was worth the comment, because Rosher so seldom did.

The inspector's brows were down, his little eyes fixed sternly ahead and rock-hard under the low brim of the black hat. "Bloody poofters," he said. He hated poofters.

7

The rest of the day was not exactly busy, but for Fisk and Rosher and for every other policeman engaged, it was wearing, as are all those days that settle into the routine plod, plod, plod with no sudden yip of eureka to make it worthwhile.

The follow-up teams had called at every one of the houses visited earlier by the house-to-house lads. The function of the follow-up team is to do exactly as the term implies: to follow up. To get themselves invited in if they can, to sit down with a cup of tea. To probe gently, to listen to answers often more full and free now that thinking time has elapsed since the sudden, unexpected, and hence unsettling doorknocker visit. And to mark out on their lists those houses, families, persons who might yield further if paid yet another visit, by ranking detectives.

On the more lively murder cases, of course, many such detectives are called upon. But all detectives are busy men—you should see their workload, in this wicked world—and Ultimate Brass cannot afford to make logjams by reassigning them unless it be strictly necessary. If the chief investigating officer needs some, he must ask for them. If he chooses not to ask, it is accepted that he and his existing team can handle it on their own.

Superintendent Fisk had, as yet, no reason to ask. He had Rosher to split the load with; and whatever men said about Rosher, and many said much, nobody could decry his dogged application of the boxy-toed footware in the interest of routine. No assisting sergeant had been assigned to him as yet, but there were plenty about. He only had to whistle.

They spent the rest of the morning separately, following up the follow-up team, calling at all the marked houses, the addresses obtained by radio from the station and ticked off with the house-to-house lists held on the knee. They went separately because these were not interviews of suspect subjects, so no supporting witness was needed; and one man alone looks and feels less overwhelming than two bulky ones together, and so is more likely to be invited in for a cupper.

Rosher worked straight through until lunchtime; and Fisk broke off only once. This was when he found himself with the shakes coming on and the constant interior weeping, intensified these days as the body chemistry adapted so that alcohol became necessary to it, threatening to engulf him. He went to his car. In it he kept a Thermos flask. Much more discreet to unscrew and fill the cap-cup than to sit there swigging out of a bottle.

He did not take a great deal. Just a cupful, sufficient to subdue the shaking. And another before he drove back to the station for lunch. On the way, he bought a packet of peppermints. He met up with Rosher in the canteen, and they discussed matters over braised steak, treacle tart to follow. As he wiped away the lingering crumbs, he said: "You'd better carry on down there. I'll stay here for a while, catch up on all the bumph. Take a sergeant if you think you'll need one."

''Uh-huh,'' said Rosher. Bugger the sergeant. Given choice, he worked alone.

They left the canteen and Fisk peeled off to his office, where another bottle waited in a locked drawer of his filing cabinet, to help him through his days when he needed it. Inspector Rosher went out to his car and drove yet again down to the canal basin—where he saw a thing happen that engaged his attention.

It did not occur at once. He had, in fact, continued with his calling, and paused for a teatime snack of café fruitcake with tea so weak as to pass between teeth richer in hue than itself (but it was cheap, representing profit on expenses), and afterwards resumed the knocking on doors, and the smiling, and the introducing of himself as Inspector Rosher, CID.

The smile, perhaps, did it (people facing it for the first time often fell back a pace), and the general bulky bow-legged gorillaness. Be that as it may, nobody asked him in, there was no putting on of kettles and dusting of the spare cup. Housewives preferred to keep him on the doorstep, so the only fluid that passed his lips was that cup taken in the café. This is most unusual. Policemen normally come from follow-up sogged down and burping. The seasoned mark convenient public lavatories in their minds before they begin. Vicars have the same problem, but the ecclesiastical bladder enlarges over the years to deal with it. And, of course, the fairy cakes Christian women are eternally baking help to soak it up.

It was five-thirty when Rosher finished with his last listed call, and he was thirsty. He thought to himself: I could murder a pint. If I call in to the Ring o' Roses, I can have one and a pie to go with it. Can check to see if anything's happened down there. Maybe Mavourneen will have thought of something.

In truth, he was doing the thing he did so often: giving himself reason not to go home. Nothing waited there but dust and dirty crockery, grease on the cooker and Turkey Steaklettes for dinner, with crinkled chips. Television after, and this on a night when choice lay between a bestseller movie about a Jewish family in the rag trade, Milwaukee way or somewhere very similar, a film about the mating habits of the fruit bat, and *A Week in the Life of Russel*

Harty. Work, however arduous or even degrading, must be better; and Rosher, professional from tenpenny-piece–sized tonsure to the thick sole of the boxy shoe, never had found his work arduous, and certainly not degrading.

He was not a drinking man, never had been; but a man may sit for a fair long time with a pint, and in chat he may learn something. He can then go back to the station, read up on all the latest bumph, confer with Ernie Fisk, if he is still there. Possibly even come down here again, because one class of people still had not been spoken to or seen: the winos and tramps and dropouts who might sleep in these old warehouses. There probably were none. But you never know, you never know.

Five minutes later he was entering the bar of the Ring o' Roses, the only customer here as yet. No sign of Mavourneen, but Mr. Chafers stood behind his bar, polishing glasses. Rosher said: "Good evening. Quiet."

"They don't come in till later," said Mr. Chafers. "They have their tea first."

"I'll take a pint to start you off. Bitter. And a pie. Pork."

He took his pint and his pie and sat down at a table by the window, overlooking the entire length of the quay—the narrowboats and transplanted cruisers; the black stump wall of the burned warehouse; the Nore-Smith firm and other buildings around, the slope, the bridge. The Rolls had vanished. Nore-Smith must have gone home, together with his office staff. Presumably, the fire-engendered tangle had been unraveled. No trucks were in sight.

Nothing animate was in sight, not even a policeman. And now the thing began to happen, as he sank beige incisors into cardboard crust.

He had thought, not seeing Knocker Davis when he arrived, that the working day for that man, as for most, was over. Knocker never did like work. But he must have been down in the bowels, because now his yachting cap appeared sticking out of the little door leading from the interior of one of the remaining narrowboats onto its small tiller deck. The rest of him followed, and he sat on the guardrail with his back to the pub, looking idly at the water;

enjoying the sunshine, perhaps relishing it the more for having missed so much of it in the old days, when if he was not viewing it between the high walls of the exercise yard, he was working mostly by moonlight. Or he might have been waiting for something. A hired boat returning, it could be.

And now Bert Humsey came out from the Nore-Smith yard, tubbing along this way. Bert had just finished a stressful and very busy day. By sheer sweat and directive ability he had brought the confusion under control. Firms who sent their own vans to collect goods got them, possibly an hour or two late but no more, and he had his short-haul drivers in, out, and away to work not so very far behind schedule. Long-haul men left later but would make up the time, this late start meaning that their permitted driving hours stretched well into the evening. And Sydney rang at five o'clock, when the foreman told him to arrive back about nine. It would be getting toward dusk by then. All the coppers were gone.

He was coming now on a trifling matter to do with his moonlighting job, carrying a small component to replace one gone erratic in the starter motor of one of the narrowboats, because with Mr. Nore-Smith's knowledge and permission, he made extra money by maintaining their simple diesel engines in his spare time. Diesel engines are very reliable, and there was no point in employing a full-time mechanic when this truck-trained wizard dwelt almost at the elbow, having workshop facilities and all. And Nore-Smith had no grumbles. To hold a first-class man these days when one drops into your lap as Bert had, you have to keep him sweet.

Knocker Davis, on the outboard side boat, looked up when the roly-poly weight stepping onto the one moored beside it against the quay moved both together, a slight stir rippling the water. He said: "Ah. There you are."

"You can say that again," said Bert, stepping from the inner boat to the outer. "Bastard." He meant, presumably, that it had been a bastard of a day; he wouldn't have been referring to Knocker's legitimacy status. Although, as a matter of record, he hit it with deadly accuracy. Surprising how many people speak in this explosive and elliptical fashion when they are browned right off.

"Yeah," the Knocker said, sympathetically. "I know what you mean." There it is again, you see. Elliptical. Always elliptical. Study the speech, it doesn't mean anything.

Bert deposited his small component on the deck beside the hatch under which the engine dwelt. About to raise this hatch, he checked, looked about him at the boat and the one next to it. He said: "Where's *Happy Lady?*"

"Gorn out, annit?" said the Knocker. "They'd booked this one, but you hadn't had a chance to fix the starter, so I swapped 'em over."

"You what?" said Bert.

"Swapped 'em over." The beginning of unease showed in the Knocker. There was something in Bert's tone, and your born underling acting on his own initiative is haunted deep down by the dread of cockup, humiliation piled on top of the daily ration of humiliation attendant upon his being alive.

"You twat!" said Bert.

"They didden mind," said Knocker. "It doan matter, we got no more bookings till tomorrer."

"You stupid twat!" said Bert, waving his fists in the air.

Now Rosher, savaging his pie and washing it down with bitter, saw all this happen. He saw the reflex defensive stiffening of his old friend Knocker in the face of Bert's forceful mouthing and suddenly waving fists. But of course, he could hear not a word of the dialogue. He couldn't hear Bert say: "You fucken idiot! What time'd she go out?"

"'Smawnin'," said Knocker. "After I had me dinner." They have dinner in the middle of the day, the Knocker classes. Who is to say they are not well advised? Leave it till the evening, some other bastard might eat it.

"Which way'd they go?"

Punters have a choice of cruising ground, you see. To the left, more of the town but then straight on into the beautiful country, three days as far as the loop canal. One day in the loop and back.

A week, all told, and highly recommended. To the right, under the bridge and into the country almost immediately; but a day's cruise brings you to the big city, where most people moor for the night at the quay belonging to a firm that fills you up with oil and checks your stern gland before you move on. Also highly recommended, if you like a day of viewing the city from an unusual angle before regaining the country. Some do, some don't.

"That way." Knocker pointed to his left. Rosher saw him do it.

"You prat, you prat, you stupid prat!" said Bert. His fists were balled and moving, he looked as though he might punch the poor Knocker straight over the side and into the canal. And Rosher saw this, too.

Some are born brave, but then again, many are not. Knocker had backed to the well-burnished rail, eyes bulging. "I ayn done nuffin," he said. "What'd I do? I ayn done nuffin."

Bert was not listening. He had turned and was going ashore, leaving his engine component lying on the deck. He reached the quay and began to twinkle his little roly-poly legs along it, aiming them for the pub where Rosher sat grinding pie-meat between mighty molars and watched him come.

He arrived with haste, straight in through the door; and when he saw the inspector sitting there, muscular jaw rotating slowly under the black hat and stern little eyes fixed upon him, he checked and said: "Ah."

"'Evening," Rosher said. Bert hesitated, as if to give him time to add "All," to complete the classic copper's salutation. But he didn't. That was all he said. "'Evening."

"Ah, yeah," said Bert. "'Evening." And he addressed Mr. Chafers, who stood polishing glasses still in front of all those twinkling bottles. "Er—has—um—Sydney been in? Not Sydney, Georgie." Disconcerted, he amended the name without considering that only he knew that Sydney was supposed to be, at this very moment, on his long way back from Ripon.

Rosher glanced at the bar. Mr. Chafers had his eyes down, paying attention to his work. He brought them up briefly, to say: "No. Nobody's been in, only this gentleman." Down went the eyes again and he polished assiduously.

"Ah. Ta," said Bert. He left less hurriedly, going not to the boat where Knocker stood, but along to his yard. While he was going, Rosher finished his pie and swallowed the last of his bitter. He stood up, saying to the landlord: "Funny little feller."

"Uh-huh," said Mr. Chafers.

"No Mavourneen tonight?"

"Expect she's got held up with her mum."

"Yeah. Well, don't water the beer."

The inspector left. Knocker Davis was leaving his boat now. Even at a distance he looked shaken. Rosher intercepted him as he made for the way out from the quay into the council estates. "'Evening, Knocker," he said jovially.

"Oh—Mr. Rosher," said Knocker. "Yeah. Hello, Mr. Rosher." He did not wish to linger, you could see it. Never had, when faced unexpectedly with Rosher.

"What was that all about?"

"What?"

"The little tubby feller. On the boat."

"Oh. Yeah." Once, Knocker would have denied by reflex tongue action that there was a little tubby feller; or, in his day, even a boat. But shaken now and aggrieved, he said: "I dunno, I ditten do nuffin. Bleeden mad, he is. Just corse I sent a bleeten boat orf. That's me job, ayn it?"

"Yeah, well," said Inspector Rosher, "I should try not to aggravate him. Did he say why it mattered?"

"Not a bleetin dicky. Just called me a prat, he did." Dicky. Dicky-bird. Rhyming slang for word.

"Observant little bugger, isn't he?" Rosher bared the teeth. "All right, Knocker, off you go. Don't step in anything."

The Knocker scuttled away. Rosher, watching him vanish, thought: Funny. If little Tubso had something to say about the business, some query, why didn't he come straight out with it, in the pub? And Chafers—he owns the boats. He didn't make the right reactions.

Things like that intrigued Inspector Rosher. He pulled his walkie-talkie out from the inside pocket of the durable blue serge suit with the button fly and the reinforced cuffs; remembered it was still on the blink. Never mind, there was a telephone booth up by the bridge.

Bert Humsey did not go to his office. He went right past it, through the gate in the wall that separated the transport yard from the little dead-end street where Sydney's truck had rested last night. Fifty, sixty yards along he glanced around like a furtive character in an old silent movie and vanished through the small back door of the warehouse where Clovis and Peter had their shop. He needed to hurry along a passage between wooden partition walls and down a flight of steps to find them.

They had scrubbed down the old basement walls and were applying emulsion paint, both dressed in one of those boutique boilersuits, both smoking a joint, Clovis through a long jade holder. He stood on paint-splashed steps and suspended his slapping as Bert appeared, to say: "What the hell do you want?"

"That fucken Knocker," Bert said. "He's sent the wrong bloody boat off."

"So?"

"*Happy Lady*. He's sent it off."

"Oh, Christ. With the gear on it?"

"'Course it was bloody on it. Been on since night before last, annit? Couldn't get at it—couldn't get it away."

"You stupid sod," said Clovis. "You just *left* it there?"

"Couldn't go near it, could I, for Christ's sake? Fucken coppers and firemen all over the place. I didn't know the twat was going to do it, he switched the bloody punters over from *Happy Wanderer*. I was going to take the plugs out of *Lady*, so she couldn't move."

"Why didn't you?"

"Couldn't get down there. Been bloody chaos all day, annit? Would've looked bloody suspicious, walking off the job to fuck about with bloody boats. Nore-Smith's been farting around all the time."

"You could have done it before you *started* work."

"Don't be a twat—coppers and bloody firemen all standing there? That bloody gorilla was down here eight o'clock."

"Inspector Rosher. *Bastard,*" said Clovis. "Does Chafers know?"

"I went to tell him. Just now. The bloody ape's in there, too. Eating a bloody pork pie."

Peter put a word in. He had a small and rather pretty lisp. "You silly sod," he said. Not quite thilly thod, but not so far from it.

"Be *quiet,* Peter," Clovis commanded. He came down from his ladder and stood for a moment, thinking. The pungency of pot hung on the air. He said: "If they call in at Gray's Wharf overnight, it might be all right. Benny may realize there's been a cockup and get the stuff out." *Happy Lady,* you see, should not have been arriving at the mooring in the city until tomorrow, a phone call ensuring the right reception. This was standard procedure. Never mind what holidaymakers were aboard, as soon as they were gone ashore the matter was attended to.

"They went the other way," Bert told him. Of them, because although Peter was not saying much he was there, wasn't he?

"What time did it go?" Clovis asked.

"Before he had his dinner. He said."

"They can't have got all that far." Three miles an hour, the boats are governed down to. Authority insists, because of the banks and the wild fowl who of one accord stop laying and pull out all their feathers if you do not chug sedately by. "You'll have to get after them. We can't leave it floating about for a week."

"*I* can't get after 'em," Bert said. "I've got Sydney coming back in at nine, he's got another load aboard." The two poufs knew this but he reminded them anyway. He added, "Besides, how am I supposed to get on the fucken boat? Say excuse me, don't bother to move, and start fucken unscrewing?"

"They go to pubs, in the evening," Clovis said. "We get them in here, they tell us all about it."

Peter spoke again. "The Mellow Duck. That's where they go, on the first night. The brochure puffs it."

Bert said: "You'll have to go. On your scooters. While I get Sydney in."

"Wait, wait, wait. Let me think." Clovis stood frowning for a while, puffing on the joint in his long, elegant holder. Peter, too, increased his puffing rate. Bert simply stood there, waiting.

In his pub, as soon as Inspector Rosher left, Mr. Chafers put down the glass he was polishing and went through to the living room, where Mrs. Chafers was just settling in front of the television for her nightly fix of *Crossroads,* followed by *Coronation Street*. She never budged from here until *Crossroads* and *Coronation Street* were over. He said: "Bert came belting in."

"Big deal," she snapped. A phrase she picked up from the younger element, Saturday nights in the bar. And she snapped because for many years, this was the way she had addressed him.

"He looked all worked up."

"What about?"

"He didn't say."

"Didn't you ask him?"

"The copper was in, that Rosher. He asked if Sydney or Georgie had been in, and shot straight out again." He pondered for a second, chewing his Olde Tyme Music Hall mustache. "Wonder what he wanted? He only said that when he saw the copper."

"Why don't you go and ask him, for Gawd's sake? He's only over the road."

"I'm not going over there. Not with the coppers hanging about."

She couldn't drum him for that. The entire enterprise operated under the strict rule that those concerned paid no extraneous visits to each other.

"You could say it was something to do with the boats. He's stayed on to work on the boats, hasn't he?" Fool, her tone added.

"Not with coppers around," he said firmly. "He'd had a go already with Knocker. I saw it through the window. So did the copper, I could see him watching."

"Copper, copper," she snapped. "You've got coppers on the brain."

"I don't like it," he said. "Bloody fire's made it dodgy. I don't even know if the stuff's on the boat, haven't had a chance to check with Bert. I don't like it hanging about, I don't like not knowing what's going on."

"Go and find out, then."

"Not with that bloody copper piddling about," said Mr. Chafers. "He'll be wondering what Bert was up to already. He ought to have thought of something better than that, Bert did. He didn't ought to have come rushing in and out all sweaty, coppers wonder about things like that."

"*That* copper?" said Mrs. Chafers, derisively. "Only thing he'd wonder about was they ripe if you gave him a bunch of bananas."

She was not the first to underestimate the man, and all because of the gorilla look.

8

Mr. Fisk had not been idle during the afternoon. Nor had he been entirely teetotal. When he went into his office, he closed the door carefully and unlocked the drawer in which he kept his bottle. Two fair slugs later and feeling much better, he sat down to work; not on the current case, there was nothing to be done with that for the moment, but on the paperwork accumulating around his other cases. Even when he is assigned to a murder case, a detective must snatch every opportunity offered to keep it all under control. If he doesn't, when he is free to take it up again he will find himself hopelessly snowed under. In theory, of course, he hands it all over when he is snatched away. But in practice life is not so simple. Every detective is closely bound up with enterprises that only he can handle. And as this applies to senior rank, they will all be major cases that must not be cocked up. If they are, it blots his book regardless.

His problem now was that he found it difficult to concentrate. The policeman, contrary to popular belief, is not excused the trauma and tragedy endemic to living, and normally when it comes, he copes as most men do: by beating it down to manageable proportion, aided by concentration upon his work. But there comes a point in extremis where the balance topples and personal woe refuses to be relegated. And then, if a man has been using liquor to dull the intolerable ache, there is also bottle-blur; which he will invariably try to clear by another little drink, to resharpen his focus. It's a vicious circle.

So, Mr. Fisk sat there all the afternoon fighting three battles. One: against the pain returning as the slugs wore off. Two: against the twitching temptation to pull out the cork again. Three: to forget the other two, and concentrate, concentrate, until he realized that even this praiseworthy effort was coming between him and his work. His mind was engaged on fighting itself now, and this destroyed concentration completely. He needed to clear the blur.

So he stepped again into the vicious circle. Unwillingly, knowing it was not what he used to do. But what the hell—he couldn't sit here forever getting further and further into the mire. If you can't cope with your work, it still keeps mounting up until in the end they take it away from you. And things were no longer the way they used to be, when drinking was a pipe going in a happy bar, and gregarious laughter. What the hell.

He was not drunk when Rosher made his call from the phone booth by the bridge. Nothing like it. He was sitting straight in his chair, and men popping in, handling his cases and come to seek guidance, saw nothing wrong with him. No bottle, either; between shots it went back into his desk. But he had passed from the initial blur through his time of finer focus to a more comfortable blur. The switchboard policelady told him who was calling. When she connected them, he said: "Hello, Alf. Anything?"

Receiver to hairy ear, Inspector Rosher thought: Alf? He called me Alf. He doesn't call me Alf. Pissed again, is he? Surely not. What, after this morning? He said guardedly, waiting for the other man to clarify his condition in further talk: "Nothing much. I've seen some people, finished the follow-up."

"Good, good," the superintendent said, out of his aching blur. "That's the ticket. Anything I ought to know about?"

I don't think he's pissed, Rosher thought. But then again, I don't think he's not.

He had intended, when he made for the phone, to detail quite fully his afternoon's work; but now he changed his mind. If the silly bugger *was* pissed again, there was no point. A man schickered is out of touch in his thinking, you can't pick over with him all the essential nitty-gritty. He can do the wrong things, he can issue the wrong orders—to *you,* if he is ostensibly Guv'nor. And if he lands himself in the steaming heap, you can find yourself right in there beside him, perhaps for not referring the matter to Higher Up, if you had reason to believe he might be bottled.

Cagily, the inspector said: "Not really. I'll be putting the report in." On paper. Get it down in black and white. You can't beat it.

"Good. Good. Coming back, are you?"

"Got another call to make first."

"Right. Good. I'll be here if you need me." And Mr. Fisk put the phone down.

Mr. Rosher came out from the phone booth, to lope again down the slope and along the quay. He was on his way to visit Mavourneen's house; partly, in truth, for old time's sake, because the big lady's defection from duty suggested that the condition of the Widow O'Hara might have delayed her, and he felt himself nurturing the viper of nostalgia in his fur-pelted bosom, whispering that he didn't want her to die; and partly to have further traffic with the young man Mulcahy.

He reached the quay proper just as Mr. Chafers emerged from his pub, this man having decided at last that he *had* to visit Bert, coppers or no coppers, and they all seemed to be gone. So out he came. Then, seeing the barrel-chested, black-hatted figure swinging bum-out toward him, he popped back in again like an agoraphobic weather-house man scalded by sudden rain.

In the warehouse basement, Clovis was saying: "It's the only thing we *can* do, duckie. We can't just *leave* it, floating about for a *week.*"

"But they might not get *off* the silly boat," Peter said, and not for the first time. Bert was saying nothing now. It had been agreed that he could not go, he must stay to deal with Sydney. "Not *everybody* gets off, you know, they don't *all* go mad first night."

But most, of course, do. Elevated by a long day's freedom, coaxed by brochure and guidebook, they moor by the weir along from the thatched and delightful Mellow Duck (which used to be the Navigation, but *that* won't attract tourists), where they sit and sup until closing time. They even buy pints for aged yokels, who attend on a rota system, all dressed up for it and leaving their teeth at home. It's the fairest way, the landlord says; they'd ruin the market all crowding in at once.

"They do if they're not teetotal," said Clovis. He was getting mad, it showed in the eyes and the quivering nostrils.

"They might *be* teetotal," his friend said. Quite reasonably; many people are.

"Then they'll go for a *walk,* won't they? If they don't drink, they go for a *walk.*"

True again. The brochure and the guidebook both suggest that non-topers might well rejuvenate their leg muscles, withered after a whole day of idleness, by walking to the top of the hill for the sake of the famous view. On high summer evenings that hill is liberally besprinkled with teetotalers, all gazing outward. He knew what he was talking about, Clovis did.

"They may not *go* for a walk," said Peter. "They might be *crippled* or something."

"Then we'll have to think of something else, won't we, duckie?" his friend snapped. "We can't just *leave* it floating *about,* can we?"

On the quay side of the building Inspector Rosher was passing by, directing the boxy soles toward the Ring o' Roses, where a left turn onto the exit street would bring him out to the council estates. Mr. Chafers, from back behind his bar, watched him approach, saw him make the turn, and sighed with relief. But he did not go out again. The bastard might be hiding there, ready to pop out from behind the Gents. He was all over the bloody place.

Inspector Rosher had, in fact, passed on, to reach Mavourneen's house almost before the landlord had downed a stiffening whisky and drawn himself another. The house seemed quiet enough. He knocked upon the door, faintly surprised to know that he would be sorry if the wicked old bat was dead. Mavourneen, when she answered, said: "Oh—Mr. Rosher. Come in."

He removed the black hat, worn for so long by now without a break that it left a red girdle on the leathery brow. Forensic might even have found the maker's name in reverse, somewhere under the short side hair. They can do wonders. "Good evening," he said, stepping inside. "How's your mother?"

"Quieter," she told him. "Much quieter. Were you wishing to see her?" And before he had time to say yea or nay, she had opened the living room door.

The Widow O'Hara sat in there, in the company of Irish women. No mistaking the six short noses, the wide mouths, the blue eyes all turned this way to see who was coming in. Family. Stern, they looked at this time, and they all held Guinness in a glass, the bottles set beside them. The Widow O'Hara had a Guinesss and she sat like a wizened Queen Victoria throned in an armchair, clad in black bombazine. If it was not bombazine, what on earth was it? "Ah," said Rosher, into the silence. "Good evening. Just called to—er—see how you were, Mrs.—er—O'Hara." He could hardly call her Nellie. Some of these women could, would, be her children, last seen by him when they *were* children.

The Widow O'Hara made no answer. She did not even glance at him, she just sat there looking straight ahead and clutching her Guinness. One of the other women spoke. He might have run her in, too, in her bobby-sox days. "How would she be, poor ting, wid her own flesh and blood cold and stiff in te mortuary?" Some of the younger ones he might have chased as children.

"Cold and stiff," keened the Widow O'Hara suddenly. "Cold and stiff." She took a swig at her Guinness.

Mavourneen closed the door. "I hope you were not wanting to ask her anything," she said. "I don't think she's up to answering."

"No, no," he said. "Just—er—thought I'd look in, see how

she was. I was in at the pub, you weren't there, I thought perhaps. . . . Rrrmph."

"I thought I'd better stay with her for a while. She's all right now, the girls are with her and she's got her Guinness. I'll go in for the last hour, there's not much doing till then. If I don't, himself will hang on to the money."

"Uh-huh," he said. "I'll have a word with young Mulcahy, while I'm here."

"I'm afraid you won't. He had his tea and went straight out."

Understandable. No place for him here, at present. "Ah," said Inspector Rosher.

"Was it something special?"

"No, no. Just the routine."

"You certainly work at it, don't you?" she said. "You've had a long day of it." Suddenly her voice was warmer even than her normal soft tone, and her eyes were . . . melting, tender? "I always thought you were the best of them, even when I was a little girl."

"Ah," he said. "Mm. We have to keep at it, you know. Whoever did it, he's not going to come looking for us."

"I'm sure if there's a man to catch him, you are the man himself." She was smiling at him with that new look in her eye, and in the small narrow passage the formidable bosom seemed to be looming nearer.

"Well," he said. "Mmm. I'll be getting along, then. If you—er—think of anything—yes. Well, thank you for your cooperation. Good evening."

"Good evening, Mr. Rosher," she said softly. And when he was through, she closed the door gently behind him.

He thought as he walked away: Bloody hell. Was she. . . ? She was, you know. Bugger that. I've had enough of that. He went back to his car and drove away to the station. It was after ten when she rang.

At nine o'clock, give or take a few minutes, Sydney arrived as instructed. He had stopped long enough on his way back from the big city to phone Bert, who had already prowled the canal basin and purlieus to make sure no coppers were lurking. Especially Rosher. "Come in," Bert said. And so Sydney arrived when night was descending, without a hiccup, and the foreman directed him neatly, backward, into the yard. Swinging down from his cab, the driver said: "Sod that, I bin hanging about all bloody day."

"Well," said Bert, "you got another couple of hours to do."

"Whaddaya mean?" Sydney was immediately truculent. "Let's get the bleetin stuff orf, get out of it. I've had e-fucking-nough."

"Not yet, you twat," Bert snapped. There were tight nerves around the area tonight. "Wait till the pub turns out. We don't want no piss-artists wandering in." It has been known for a toper under stress to turn aside into the yard entrance alleyway. Dirty beasts, you'd think they'd use the facilities provided before they leave the pub. Dammit, they're only just around the back and they smell quite pleasantly, with a strawberry flavor. It's the disinfectant.

"Sod that," Sydney said again. "Where we gonna wait then, for Christ's sake? Not in the bleetin office?"

"In the truck," said Bert. "We get in and close the doors."

"Sod that. I need a drink."

Bert considered. He, too, needed a drink. Well, there was no risk in it. Was there? Long-haul drivers coming in late often went to the pub for a drink, and often he went with them. And he did want to slip a word to Chafers, see if he knew what was going on. He couldn't do it overtly with Sydney at his elbow because Sydney, mere underling, had no idea the landlord was involved in anything but serving as his license permitted. But it should be possible, perhaps while ordering at the bar with Sydney at a table, to whisper privately back and forth. And by God, it had been a helluva day, not over yet. If ever a man needed a drink. And Sydney needed stiffening, he was coming apart. Bert made up his mind.

"All right. We'll go across to the pub. But no getting tanked, mind. One round, and that's it."

"Yeah, yeah, yeah," the driver said, irritably impatient. "Let's go and get it, then, for Christ's sake."

Mavourneen was there when they got to the Ring o' Roses,

come in to serve the last hour or so. Drinkers were here, too, quite a clutch of them. She thought nothing of it when the two men arrived and threaded their way to the bar, where Bert—too many people around for a furtive mutter with Chafers, and Sydney moored alongside—ordered a double Scotch for himself and brandy, another double, for the driver. Even when, passing close by two or three minutes later, she heard Sydney call for the same again, her mind hardly registered the thought that they'd sunk those doubles pretty quick.

It gave a small kick when only minutes after that Sydney asked Mr. Chafers, behind the bar by now, for a half-bottle to take away, and the two men departed leaving more empty glasses. But she did not really start thinking until ten minutes later, when Clovis arrived in his leather jacket, crash helmet in hand. She saw him come in; she saw Chafers flick an eye toward the little private bar next door, used only for overflow on busier nights than this and entered from outside by a separate door. She saw Clovis leave at once, without even coming in properly. She saw Mr. Chafers slip unobtrusively away. That's when she started to think.

Clovis drove his motor scooter, with Peter riding pillion, a mile along the main road and then through the lane that leads to and over a humpy bridge spanning the canal. On one side of this bridge stands the Mellow Duck, nicely named for nighttime, when soft amber light glows at the curtained windows. On the other side are the three-tier locks above which the boats tie up. It doesn't take long to get there on wheels. You can cover in twenty minutes on fairly straight tarmac as much distance as a governed-down boat will in a full day of meandering along the twisty waterway.

They coasted down to just short of the bridge, where there is a layby–cum–car park for the benefit of tourists, for this is a noted beauty spot, and walked the few yards to where the trees end and you can see both ways along the canal. A lovely night, soft and starry; and no moon yet. Enough light, though, for Clovis to say very softly (there was nobody about, but people engaged in nefarious enterprise normally speak softly): "There it is—look—at the top of the locks."

"How do you know that's it?" Peter said. The boat could not be seen all that clearly. "It might be another one."

"We'll go and find *out,*" said Clovis. Under strain, they snapped and snarled at each other, obviously, like any other husband and wife when the billing and cooing is over.

"They might be on it."

"If they *were,* they'd be showing lights, duckie."

"They might be in bed."

"Oh, for heaven's *sake,*" said Clovis. "We'll go and find *out.*" And he moved toward the towpath; paused to unbuckle his helmet, whispering back to Peter, "Take your crash hat off." This was sensible of him. If anything did go wrong, no point in advertising that you came by motorbike, with pretty flowers painted all over your head.

It was the *Happy Lady,* occupying front-runner position, right up to the lock with only one other boat behind. Clovis made his whisper. "There you are. And there's nobody on it."

Certainly, there were no lights showing behind the windows. But Peter said again: "They might be in bed or something."

"They're *not,*" hissed Clovis. "They're *out.*"

"There'll be somebody on the other one."

"There *won't.*" The other boat was as dark as this. "Come *on,* for God's sake. We're wasting *time.*" He was fumbling in his leather jacket for the key handed to him by Bert, in the warehouse earlier. The roly-poly man kept keys for each of the boats, to facilitate maintenance work and the odd very private job he needed to do. "Get the screwdriver out."

Peter in turn fumbled beneath his jacket, looking around nervously as he did so. Nobody seemed to be about. Nothing stirred, not even the leaves on the trees cloaking the looming hill behind them. No breeze to rustle them. By the time he held the screwdriver in his hand, Clovis was on board and had unlocked the door leading to the boat's interior, whispering: "Come on, come on."

"You do it," said Peter.

"*You'll* have to do it." Quite obviously, the bigger man was as twitchily nervous as his friend. "You're *smaller.*" And as the lad held back: "Oh, for God's *sake!* Do you want to be here forever?"

Peter looked all around again before he stepped as one who treads on eggshells onto the little afterdeck. He held out the screwdriver, mutely. It wobbled. Clovis seized his shoulder roughly, urging him into the little door. "Get *on* with it, get *on* with it," he hissed.

"Ll-let me know if . . . anybody comes," said Peter.

"Get *on* with it!"

The lad ducked his head and moved on, through the narrow but pretty saloon, past the kitchen area and the shower cubicle (they do them up very well, these boats; the brochure does not lie), and through the two bedrooms, one with double bunks, to the tiny settee-seated cubicle called the Observation Salon immediately abaft the minuscule foredeck. There is nothing on this tiny deck, no room for anything more than a post for the mooring rope; but beneath it is a space, separated from the Observation Salon by a bulkhead. You need to be fairly small, or if tall a contortionist, to get at it. Peter was fairly small. So was Bert, who'd worked here lying on his side upon the settee seat, because he was roly-poly.

The bulkhead had a skirting board, an ordinary four-inch strip of wood held by screws. But behind it was a solid-steel panel fitted by Bert, with a patent lock requiring a key. Peter dealt with the screws all right, but fumbling with nerves, so that Clovis poked his head in through the door, pitching his hiss to travel the length of the boat.

"Hurry up for *God's* sake. What are you *doing* in there?"

Peter by now had uncovered the steel plate. He hissed back: "Where's the key? I haven't got the key."

Only now—it shows how extreme nervousness paralyzes the mind—did Clovis realize that he had the key, a duplicate of which rested in the pocket of one Benny Fowler, employee of that firm in the big city at whose wharf the boats often tied up overnight. It was on the little ring that held the key to the outer door. He snatched it from the lock, hissing: "Oh, for Christ's sake," and bobbed his head, to stumble through the boat.

Peter took it, used it, and began to scrabble out the fat plastic packages and the cardboard box hidden in that triangular space.

Triangular because it was, of course, a sort of safe, necessarily shaped to follow the line of the bow. By the time he had this done Clovis was back on the afterdeck, scanning all round and whispering: "Come on, come on, come on."

Peter replaced, relocked the steel. He propped up the skirting board and reaffixed one screw. That was enough—he needed to be out of here. He picked up the little packages and the cardboard box, placed the keys on top, and hurried to join Clovis. He held out the burden with hands shaking so much that when Clovis seized it, the keys and two of the packages dropped to the deck. "Pick 'em up, pick 'em up, pick 'em up," whispered Clovis, like a malevolent sergeant major with collapsed vocal chords.

Peter bent over. He handed the keys to Clovis and stood with the packages in his hands while his big friend fumbled at the lock, the cardboard box tucked under his arm. And a great voice cried: "Hey, you there!"

It was not the people who belonged to the boat. They were safely in the Mellow Duck, trying to coax the morose old countryman whose turn it was for the free pints (and he was morose because they were the only mugs in, and his next turn not until November, when nobody would be in at all) to croak them one of the old canal-builders' songs. This was the couple from the boat lying astern, who were teetotal, non-smoking, vegetarian, very fit, and loved climbing hills, which they did in voluminous shorts and fishermen's sweaters. They came down now by the path through the woods, and so did not see the two men on the *Happy Lady* until they emerged onto the towpath a mere fifty yards away when the bearded one, who would have been the male, shouted immediately: "Hey, you there!" And both began to run, the frontage of the one without the beard bucking wildly, very like twin coypus romping under a knitted blanket.

Neither Clovis nor Peter hung about. Clovis, bent to extract the key when the shout came, shot upright and was ashore in one stride, legging it for the bridge. But Peter . . . ah, Peter.

It is instinctive in the terrified when assailed to move rapidly away from the source of the assailing. So, still clutching his plastic bags, the lad went outboard. Foolish, but let he who never panicked caught burgling a boat cast the first stone. He panicked outboard, and was on the narrow side deck before he could think: Ah, the other way would have been better.

Now the bearded assailant had drawn ahead, being longer in the leg than the other and not hampered by coypus; and he chose to take off after Clovis. Had he not done so, had he leaped onto the boat, what happened next might have been circumvented. Then again, it might not. Who can tell about these things? He pounded past, shorts flapping, going faster even than Clovis, a nice performer himself over sprint distance but with the fine balance necessary for your actual record-setting disturbed by the cardboard box, still clutched under one arm. They were almost at the bridge when the beard caught up and grabbed, digging his heels in, which brought him and Clovis both slithering to a halt. But a leather jacket is slippy, and his grip broke; and Clovis, sobbing, whirled and went up in the air like Nureyev.

It was a matter of five years since he retired from his vocation as a ballet dancer, and he was never in the Nureyev class. But a person who has been thoroughly soaked in ballet dancing or riding a bicycle never loses the capacity. Up went Clovis into the air, a high-class entrechat (is it?) even in heavy biking boots—marvelous what you can do given sufficient incentive—the leading one of which flashed out and home, bap into the bearded man's whiskers.

Even this might not have stopped him. But it thickened his lip, knocked his top set right out, and cracked the bottom ones, which jumped backward into his throat. By the time he had choked them out, staggering about carefully in case he trod on the others, Clovis was gone and diversion had occurred.

Peter, scrambling among the six-inch-wide side deck, could not have reversed now, even had he thought of it. He'd always been mortally afraid of women anyway, and that was a woman, leapt aboard and crying: "Come back! Come back!" A large and looming woman, bigger than his horrible mother. Dead now, God rest her soul. He scrambled on, while she took to the side deck behind him. Risky—if she'd banged that bosom on the coachroof, it would have bounced her overboard.

Now a tiny deck with a post and a rope on it is a hazard by night. Many a weekend yachtsman has plunged to his death in the icy Solent because of one. Peter, attaining the foredeck, made to leap, over the bows and onto the shore; and of course his foot caught the rope, and him in the very air.

Even then he might have been all right, if the great top timber of the lock gate had not been slippery with new-descending dew. Because this is where he desperately landed, to teeter with arms waving, to slip, to plunge with one short, sharply cut scream into the lock. And the lock was empty.

Perhaps he saved Clovis. For the bearded man, hearing the screams and believing it might be his woman (who is thinking clearly, at a time like this? She had a yip like a pit-head hooter), left his top teeth wherever they lay and came sprinting back to find her scrambling to the lock edge, looking over. He joined her. They gazed down at Peter, spread in the mud beside the skull-shattering timbers framing the paddles, his crash helmet left on the coachroof. She said: "Is he dead?"

"I hope not," he said, as the starting up and receding of Clovis's scooter rattled the air. "I finferely hope not." Teetotal non-smoking vegetarians seldom swear, even under great duress. Nor do scoutmasters, and he was all of these.

"Why have you taken your toofies out?" she said.

9

When Mavourneen rang Inspector Rosher, her motives were mixed. Certainly, he had told her to watch for anything funny happening at the pub, and funny things were happening; but she did not really believe they bore on the matter of her nephew's death.

Although she had, be it agreed, sufficient reason to ring him, she probably would not have done so at this time of night. She'd have left it until morning, but for the mix of motives.

She was shocked and upset by the lad's death, she was enduring alone her extrovert mother's keening and the pressure of neighbors and visiting family. Such circumstances pitch a basically lonely woman into extreme emotional vulnerability. Never mind all the feminist claptrap: When a woman is hit with sudden insecurity, her mind yearns to wrap her around a man.

Well, Rosher was that, never doubt it. While all about her keened and emoted, he was fixed and firm, tough as she remembered him from her childhood, when she—among others—had had a child's crush on him.

Oh yes, and not only children fancied him in those days of his reknown as formidable fighting man, in the ring and out; especially in areas such as this had been, where a man was judged by his battle ability rather than his social urbanity. Even his gorillaness was a sexual asset rather than a liability down here, outward proof of the security he would bring to the female could she latch on to him, and strong hint of desirable stallion quality. In every primitive society woman knows it well: Good looks fade, and go often with weakness, but a man like a gorilla endureth forever.

He was older now, of course, but the aura of rampant maleness was with him still. Not altogether surprising if the fancy for him came back. And he was free—the grapevine down here buzzed at the time when he bumped suddenly down to sergeant, and buzzed again when as suddenly he reelevated to inspector. They don't forget their tough coppers, in tough districts. They take personal pride in it, when they know one who has done well and is seen from time to time on television. Terrible old bugger, he was, they tell their children admiringly. Or ould bugger, in Irish districts. So are legends born.

She rang the station on her way home, from a callbox near her house. He was not there, he was eating bread and cheese with a pickled onion in his house on the hill, across on the other side of town. Not finished for the day, even yet. Home for a meal and a clean-up. Then out again, for a prowl around those warehouses, seeking tramps, layabouts, kids sleeping rough—anybody who might shed a little light on the case of John Patrick O'Hara. "Can we help you?" they asked.

"I will only talk to himself," she said.

This is not unusual. Police stations take calls all the time from people who will speak to nobody but the copper named. Every detective has his private network. So they passed on his home phone number. Why not? Nothing secret about it, she could have got it from the directory.

"Hello," he said. "Rosher."

She did not hear this, because if you ring from a British callbox, when the number is answered, you get weep-weep-weep-weep-weep, right over the speaking, until you fumble your coin in, so you don't know who the hell it is. Wherefore, she said: "Mr. Rosher?"

"Speaking."

"Ah. Good. It's me here."

"Uh-huh," he said, and sucked a morsel of cheese out of a big brown molar. He knew who it was. Who else would deliver that soft, molded Irishness into his hairy ear?

She told him what she had seen. Bert and Sydney, rapidly despatching doubles and taking away a half-bottle; Clovis with his crash helmet, being signaled by Mr. Chafers into the little private bar. That's all there was, so it did not take long.

He said: "Uh-huh. Anything like this ever happened before?"

"No," she said. "Only last night. They were drinking doubles last night, Bert and that other one. They never drink shorts, only beer."

No real weight in any of it. Probably a load of old wallop. But he had told her to let him know if she noticed anything unusual. And you can never quite tell—when you are casting about, you cannot afford to ignore the slightest dip of the float. He was going down there anyway. Wouldn't do any harm to have a word with Chafers. Presumably, the pouf and the transport lads would have gone home by now.

"Well, thank you for ringing. Is young Mr. Mulcahy back yet?"

"I don't know, I've been working. Haven't got home meself."

"Uh-huh. Well, I'm coming down that way. I'll call again, if I may. Have a word with him."

"Don't you ever stop working?" she said. And then her time ran out and she vanished abruptly, in a welter of weep-weep-weep.

Inspector Rosher finished his snack without hurrying it and rubbed his shoes over. He had very tough feet, and the bath he had taken together with a couple of hours in slippers had eased away the long day's ache. Before he clapped on the black hat, he rang Superintendent Fisk, who had gone home from the station just before he did. Suppose I'd better, he thought, he'd better know where I am. Better be told, anyway, even if he's too pissed to absorb it.

Superintendent Fisk was not pissed. He would have liked to be, he had several more slugs taken during the evening; but his underlying solid professionalism had asserted itself, aided by the jolt it received this morning, to hold him back from complete capitulation. He was not, after all, off duty, no murder case leader ever is. Home, in compliance with the sensible rule of take a break while you can, but at the end of the telephone. And it must not be thought that while the ostensible command strata is so resting, the case is suspended. Many other men are engaged, and active.

So the superintendent had spent the evening sipping just sufficiently to maintain the slight blurring that helped him through the afternoon. It kept him steady all evening—until his wife came in.

They were in the middle of an unholy row when Rosher called. Mr. Fisk snatched up the phone and barked: "Yes?"

Surprised by the tone, Mr. Rosher said: "Ah. I'm—er—just going out. Down to the canal."

"Anything special?"

If there was one thing nobody should ever do, it was bark at Rosher. It turned his neck red, it bristled the nape. Away went his intention of sharing his little float-wobble with Ernie Fisk. Sod

Ernie Fisk. "No," he barked in return. "Just going to hunt for layabouts. As we arranged."

"All right," barked Ernie. "If you need me, let me know." Down with the phone and he turned back to his wife, barking match over. The main bout still to come.

Bert sat with Sydney in the back of the great truck, until the pub closed. He did not enjoy it, he did not approve the driver's bringing liquor back with him, but there was nothing he could do about it. A transport foreman's authority is very limited; he cannot command stern obedience as a sergeant major can. If he tries, his troops say, "Stuff you." So he sat in the back of the truck and even took a nip himself out of the bottle, all in the dark with Sydney. He had torches, lights on plug-in cables, all sorts of lamps; but you never knew whether a truck is completely chinkproof. Better not take the chance.

At ten-fifteen, he said: "They'll be closing in a quarter of an hour. Let's get the floor up."

"Can't bloody see, can we?" the driver said. He had finished his half-bottle. Perhaps it had done him the world of good, but he still sounded very snappy, very edgy. A touch of slur now, to go with it.

"We'll have to use a torch," said Bert. "Get the one out of your cab." Every truck has a big, strong torch, encased in rubber. It's standard equipment.

"You fucking get it," Sydney suggested. His bottle empty, he was running his tongue round the lip of it. Soon, he'd be sucking the cork.

Bert thought: Yeah, better not let him out, he might go nipping off for another bottle. I'd better do it. He said: "All right, hang on," and opened the great rear door; squeezed through, found the torch where it should have been, brought it back, and gave it to Sydney, saying: "Shine it about a bit. I'll have a look from outside, see if anything shows."

Nothing did. He climbed back into the truck body and spent the next ten minutes unfastening those strips of metal that cover where the metal plates forming the floor join the side walls. Not all of them, just the ones with the gear under. Good men had worked on this truck; it would have taken a very sharp eye to spot the double-skinning. Especially with a load on.

Ten minutes after Mavourneen rang Inspector Rosher, that man had belted himself into his driving seat and was on his way down from the hill. He went directly to her house, and she was waiting for him. Obviously, because she opened the door almost before his thick finger landed on the bell. "Ah, Mr. Rosher," she said. "Come inside, do."

He stepped yet again into her hall. If the ladies were still in the living room, they were keeping very quiet about it. A high, cracked singing came from upstairs. He cocked an eyebrow. She said: "It's Mother, I gave her a little extra Guinness to calm her nerves."

"Seems to have done her good," he said.

"Yes. Well, it does. I've put her into her bed. Don't make a noise, she'll be after coming down."

"Is Mr. Mulcahy back?"

"No. Not yet. I think perhaps you'd better see this." She reached into the pocket of her apron and brought forth a passport.

He flipped it open. It was British and showed the lad Mulcahy; but it called him Robert Henry Jones, and said he was born in London. He flipped on. By the stamps, the owner had made several trips, all to Amsterdam. "Where did you get this?" he asked.

"I was—er—clearing out Johnnie's room. His things. Just now. I—came across it." She hurried on. "Look at the dates, the last ones."

He looked. She came closer, to point them out. The bolster dinted softly against his arm. He noticed, and moved the arm slightly away. The bolster followed. "That last one," she said. "That's just before he moved in here."

"Uh-huh," he said. It had happened to him before, in his younger days. Women commonly signal sexual interest by soft application of the breasts, under some pretext. But he had never been a bolster man. And women do not, with a scatty old mum to see to, clear out dead youth's rooms at this time of night.

"He told me—us—he came from Coventry."

That was what he had told Rosher, who checked the stamps. The last was a departure. The one before, dated three months previously, an arrival. No departure appearing between. It looked as though the lad spent those three months in Holland. No record at all that he left it. "Mm," he said. "Yes. Interesting."

It is always of interest to a policeman, when he comes across something out of kink. There is no law forbidding your saying you come from Coventry when in fact you have been for some months in Holland. There is no law, if your name is Robert Henry Jones, prohibiting your calling yourself Brendan Mulcahy. But if your name is Brendan Mulcahy and you are a citizen of Eire, traveling on a British passport as Robert Henry Jones, then you are being very naughty, and are worthy of scrutiny. It may be that the policeman to whose attention you are drawn is working on murder, and cannot turn aside personally to scrutinize you. But he'll certainly see to it that somebody does. "Do you have a phone?" asked Rosher.

"No. There's a little box, just along the road."

"Uh-huh. I'll take this with me." He wagged the passport. "When Mr. Mulcahy comes back, don't mention it. Right?"

"I'm not daft, am I?" she said. When they were not in single file there simply was not room enough in this passage for all of them, she, her bust, and Rosher.

No, I don't think you are, he thought. And I don't think you just found this. I think you've just decided to show it. I wouldn't mind betting you know pretty well what's in the lad's kit. Most women know most things about their lodgers. Well, we can take that up later, if we need to. "Thank you," he said. "You've been most cooperative."

Her bolster gave him a nudge. "Oh, I can be," she said, "when I'm doing it with the right people."

"Ymmph," he said. "Mm. Right, then. I'll be on my way."

"Is it anything to do with Johnnie, do you think?"

"I doubt it. I very much doubt it." But it could be. Taking everything together—yes, it very well could be. He moved out from behind the bosom, and left.

The phone box was a hundred yards away, between here and the Ring o' Roses. He used it to call Superintendent Fisk. Better let him in on it. The passport matter had to be reported, and better give it to Ernie than to most. The Fisk number rang out and rang out, with nobody answering. After a while he cut it off and rang the station, to ask if Mr. Fisk was there.

"No," they said, "Mr. Fisk is at home." "Funny," Rosher said, "I've been trying to raise him. No answer."

"Maybe his phone is up the stick," they said.

"Better give the telephone people a buzz," he said. "Get 'em to test it." And he hung up, thinking: On the other hand, maybe he's passed out. Or gone out, even—left the bloody job flat, chasing up that bloody wife of his. When he finished here, he'd call at Ernie's on the way home. Take the passport with him. Even if Ernie was too pissed to remember him doing it, he'd have acted then by the book. He walked on, down to the canal basin, arriving just in time to see the landlord helped back into his pub.

It was Clovis who precipitated what had happened. It must not be thought that when he leaped into his saddle—and that can be painful, as any man who has slipped mounting a bicycle knows—and shot away on his scooter, he abandoned young Peter callously and completely. This would be a grave injustice.

He panicked, yes. His genes and very chromosomes howled for precipitate flight. But he loved that boy with the love that sways its hips and calls the beloved duckie. He had expected that Peter, flying on fear-winged feet, would arrive at the car park simultaneously with himself, or sooner. But Peter screamed, and there was a bonking squelch, and the scream cut off. They'd got him. Or something. And—oh God—their helmets still stood on the narrowboat roof.

A hundred yards or so up the lane he drove onto a track leading into the woods clothing the lower slopes of that big hill. He hid the scooter among bushes and crept down through the trees, which was brave of him.

By the time he got to where he could see what was going on, flat on his belly and peering through undergrowth, the cannon-ball–juggling lady had borne them along to the Mellow Duck and returned with the hirers of the narrowboat, called Mr. and Mrs. Pierce and not very interesting, really; and her husband had stemmed the bleeding from his thick lip. Other people came from the pub, of course, to shuffle about obscuring the line of sight.

He saw between them, though, the bearded man and another come up from the depths of the lock, climbing the metal ladder, and somehow bearing Peter between them. He saw the poor boy passed to men bending to receive him. He saw the lad laid out flat upon the towpath, and some officious fool kneel to give mouth-to-mouth resuscitation, filling him up with beer fume. He stayed a while to see if it worked. It didn't. He crept away.

He rode all the way back to town unhelmeted, which ruined his hairstyle and alone could have got him pinched. He was lucky, no policemen were about. Or perhaps he was not; a delay here might have circumvented what happened. For that matter, he could have gone straight to the flat in town that he shared with Peter. But he came back to the yard. To Bert, to Chafers, the men who must share his burden. Motivated by a need deeper than thought, blindly seeking the only company he could seek, in his condition of utterly lonely shock. It is a rare man who can cope with shock all alone.

Bert and Sydney had just taken up the necessary sections of the truck flooring to reveal the flattish wooden trays when he came scooting into the yard, hair all spiked as lacquered hair will, hit too hard by a headwind. They use these trays in Holland when they transport tomatoes, but now they were sheathed in black plastic. As Sydney prized the first few out—there were two dozen of them under there—Bert got down from the truck to open the back doors. And Clovis came blinding into the yard, to let his scooter fall and to stumble wild-eyed and spiky across, crying:

"Oh—oh—he's dead, he's dead, he fell in the lock!"

Bert shoved the door closed. "Who fell in the lock?" he demanded, and he was badly shaken. As who would not be? Inside the truck, Sydney froze with his heart jumping like a guppy beset by sudden piranha fish.

"He fell in the lock, he fell in the lock!" Clovis cried. He was actually wringing his hands. "Peter fell in the lock!"

There were cogent reasons why Bert should get him out of the way. Firstly, his arrival and condition were a terrible shock, piled on top of tension; and terribly dangerous, the sudden caterwauling out here. Secondly, Sydney knew nothing of the enormity of the operation, he believed that only he and Bert were involved, working a private enterprise. He didn't know about Clovis, Peter, Chafers, and all the rest. He was chicken enough to panic right now. He'd be away like the wind—and possibly to the police, if only to clear himself—if he got onto the larger matter. So Bert said: "Shut up—inside!" He then spoke through the truck door. "Start getting 'em in, Sydney. I'll be back in a minute."

"What's up, what's up?" said Sydney. "Where you fucking going? What's up?" He'd heard the urgent voices all right; but the interior acoustics of an aluminum-sided truck are very peculiar. Sounds from within are greatly magnified. Words from without do not carry.

"Nothing, nothing," said Bert. "Accident, that's all. Up at the lock. Get the stuff in. Nothing to do with us." He closed the door again, turned to grab weeping Clovis by the arm. "Come on," he said, and hauled him away thorugh the gate into that little street, through the warehouse door, and on to the prettily decorated shop. Not into the basement, where the gear was to be stored. Sydney must not find this cream-puff gibbering there when he arrived with trays.

Sydney, in fact, was urgently considering immediate flight; but look at the bloody floor, up now and with all the boxes exposed to whatever gaze happened to peek in. He couldn't even lock the truck, Bert had got the key. He, too, in his time of sudden loneliness, yearned to be near Bert. He picked up the four boxes he had stacked and descended to the cobbles, using his broad back to close the doors before he set off trotting for the warehouse, just as

Mr. Chafers's need to know what was happening brought him at last from his pub, the drinkers all gone and the bar lights extinguished. All these stresses, all these things happening at once. And something else, too. At just about this time, a sharp thrust at a shoulder sent Mr. Fisk tumbling down the stairs in his house on the nice side of town.

10

The row between the Fisks was no worse than many they had had in the past. The barbs were more shrewdly aimed now than in earlier days, because skill increases with practice. Her aim in particular had come to perfection by the honing of natural talent. Hell hath no fury like the talented shrew; she can work herself up to murder.

He was, by now, drunker than he might have been. She was out, as usual, when he arrived home; and when she came in, not long before Rosher's call, it was to change her dress. Somebody had spilled soup down the one she had on. Cool as you please, she came in and said she was back to change her dress, and that she was going out again, to the Blue Devil Club. Didn't offer even to cook him something. Not so much as a bean on toast.

Truly, is it any wonder he snarled at her? He was standing on the ground where peace of mind used to be, despite the roaring of ebullient sons. The carpet was grubby now, the furniture, the very pictures on the wall shone once with his loved wife's attention, that settee was the same one on which he sat beside her, smoking his pipe with innocuous beer at his elbow while they watched the moving pictures on the same television. The color, that wife had always said, was too blue. It never bothered him.

There was no such peace with this wife. He came up the stairs behind her into the bedroom where she changed her dress, shouting at her, accusing her of having other men. Because soup down a dress means dinner, and company at it, probably horseplay; and if she dined out and troubled to dress for it and to change when that dress became less than perfect there'd be a man, paying and no doubt waiting now, in the Blue Devil Club.

Well, she didn't deny it. She snarled right back at him. Other men? So? He wasn't to think there weren't plenty in the queue, and she didn't get much out of him, did she? Three months since she got anything at all.

And that was true. Increasing abhorrence of the woman reduces a man to incapacity. And over the long term, alcohol plays the false friend in sex as in everything else.

When Rosher called, he snatched up the extension phone standing on the bedside cabinet—even that cabinet his first wife chose—and barked: "Yes?"

The voice coming out of the phone was Rosher's. He sounded surprised by the bark, almost disconcerted. Mr. Fisk did not really notice. "Ah. I'm—er—just going out. Down to the canal."

"Anything special?" Another bark.

And now the phone barked in return. "Just going to hunt for layabouts. As we arranged."

"All right," barked Fisk. "If you need me, let me know." Down with the phone, and he turned back to his wife. Leaving Rosher saying sod you, mate.

She had zipped, and really she looked remarkably attractive in a deep blue dress that showed a reasonable quota of cleavage. He remembered that dress, from back before he married her. That, or one very like it. She was turning toward the door as he finished his bark with Rosher. He slammed the phone down and beat her to the head of the stairs where he stationed himself, arms spread so that she could not squeeze by, shouting: "You're not bloody going, don't think it. You're bloody well staying here!"

And this from the laconic, equable Ernie Fisk, the well-bottomed puffer upon a reliable pipe. These qualities, of course, are the very ones that arouse contempt, once their novelty has worn off, in the shrew-woman who equates strength with violent disturbance.

She said: "*Out* of my way!" and hit him on the shoulder with the heel of her hand. Well, he went backward. Teetered for a moment, arms waving, then tumbled backward, head over heels, all the way down the stairs. He lay at the bottom huddled and still, face down to the hall carpet. And she came down the stairs, stepped right over him, and left the house without a backward glance.

Edwin Chafers scanned the ground carefully through the pub window before venturing forth. It is possible that he would have stayed within despite his need to know. But he twittered so much to his snap-dragon wife that in the end she nettled him into it. "What are you?" she demanded, "man or bloody mouse? Go and hide under the bloody bed, *I'll* go and see 'em."

He snapped back at her; but he went now. Came out from his darkened pub, looked furtively around, and hurried along the quay, turning into the haulage-firm yard entrance. The truck stood there, alone and silent. No Sydney, no Bert; but he knew where they must be. Clovis had told him earlier where the stuff was to be stored, now that the old place had been burned down. In part, his unrest was due to the fact that Clovis should have reported back by now, with the narrowboat cargo recovered. And there'd been no sign of him. Perhaps he was with Bert.

What were they doing about Sydney? Sydney shouldn't be here, he was on the outside of the big stuff.

He moved on, to the warehouse. Had he not paused at the truck, he would have seen Sydney ahead of him, bearing his second batch of boxes in.

Unsettled though Sydney was, and a little whoozed from his half-bottle, he nevertheless was attending faithfully to his end of the enterprise. He had to, and he knew it. Things could not be left as they were, truck floor up and everything on display. Cursing Bert, he had carried one batch of trays into the cellar and returned for more. Clear the truck, drop the floor back into position. Screw it home, and Bert or no Bert, he'd be away.

Where *was* bloody Bert? *He* should be here; together they always finished the offloading in a couple of runs. Tell you one thing, his overstretched and raging mind said, it's the last fucking lot *I* run in. Not worth the sodding candle.

Nobody had told him to cover the trays, or with what. If anybody knew just how or where they were to be hidden down here, it was the vanished Bert. He flashed his torch around—a right idiot he'd have been to switch on the light—and it showed the painting gear left here by Clovis and Peter, one big dust-sheet heaped by the pots and rollers. He used it to cover the trays and was almost at the door on his way back to the truck when he heard footsteps.

He thought for a second that it must be Bert; but the steps were hesitant, the feet feeling their way. And now they were coming down the stairs.

Fear. It eliminates constructive thought, it sets the mind entirely on itself. The bent dread discovery. Particularly they dread the police. Sydney's mind told him he had been watched. Followed. It said he was lumbered, all on his own and red-handed. He got behind the door, heart choking him. It was the fucking fuzz.

Chafers should have spoken names, however guardedly. It might at least have suggested to Sydney that he was some sort of acquaintance, even though he had no idea anybody else was involved. But the unknown man hissed, as he came through the door, "Anybody there?" And Sydney hit him, right across the face with his big, heavy torch. He lurched against the wall as the driver sprang out, brought the torch up, and smashed it down again. A great rubber-covered torch makes a beautiful cosh. Down went Edwin Chafers with one little grunt; and Sydney tramped right over him with his big heavy boots in the panic of his getting away.

Bert, closeted with the sobbing Clovis in the shop, heard him go. He was making no effort to muffle the beat of his feet over bare boards. Clovis's wet eyes came up, focused with fear. The foreman said: "It's all right, it's all right." He listened a while, stiffened like a pointer. Silence. He said: "You stay here." And he crept with beating heart through the door.

He certainly could not stay where he was, he had to know what was going on. And there was no sound now, no hint that anybody was about. Creeping close to the wall, he inched toward the cellar, where in the dark he stepped on Mr. Chafers's fingers, as the man rose onto hands and knees. "Oo Christ," said Mr. Chafers, groggily. "Oo, bloody hell."

There was good stuff in Bert. Lesser men—cite Sydney as example—might well have panicked. But Bert's mind, sharpened rather than blinded by fear, recognized the voice even as his boot swung back to kick whoever it was senseless. He said: "Mr. Chafers?"

"Oo Christ," said Mr. Chafers again. "What happened?"

Bert knew what had happened. Never mind the details, to his racing mind the outline was clear. He fumbled for his cigarette lighter. Its flickering flame showed Chafers indeed, on hands and knees, wringing his trampled fingers and moaning. "What the fuck are you doing here?" he said.

"Oo Christ," said Mr. Chafers. "Oo. Oo, bloody hell." And he sagged full length on the floor.

Three minutes later, Bert helped him back to his pub. Again: What else could he do? The man could not be left there, there was only one place to take him. No good even trying to explain anything, he appeared to be concussed. He left knowing no more than he knew when he arrived, and in much worse shape, with blood all over his chin and shirt front from a mashed nose and one arm lugged over Bert's shoulder. He'd never have made it alone, his feet simply would not co-exist.

Roly-poly Bert might be, and curiously bent; but give him this, he was the one man with guts enough to try to swim them all against a sea of troubles. Thus, he did not overlook the danger of simply leaving Clovis alone in the shop. Sydney on the loose, panicked; Peter perhaps dead. All he needed was this pouf rushing forth weeping all over the place. He might even have to be eliminated. But not now. For now, keep him in. There was a key in the door. He went up, said to Clovis: "Stay here. I'll be back in a minute."

"Where are you going?" Clovis demanded. Weeping still, dabbing his eyes with a pretty hankie.

"Got to help Sydney get the truck straight," said Bert, and on his way out he locked the door. Never tell a panicking man that other men have panicked. It can turn the man into a running, bleating sheep.

Now he slung Chafers's arm over his shoulder and began to transport him back along the quay, with great difficulty because the publican was a deal taller than he. He was almost up to the Ring o' Roses when he realized that the shop had another door, and Clovis probably had the key.

No time to think about that now. He pressed on, anxious to have this foot-sagging body off his back and under cover. All seemed quiet enough; but you never know who might be about.

Indeed, you do not. Inspector Rosher was about, come through that little street leading from the council estate. Well shadowed at night, the little street, and he had just stepped into deeper shadow, saying to himself, Allo-allo—what's going on?

Sydney, by this time, had reached home. Before his little wife had time to say where the hell have you been, as the best of wives will when her husband comes in late showing signs of heavy weather, he had said: "I've been here all the evening. Haven't even bin out. Right?"

"What you been up to?" she demanded. Curlers in her hair, little pink dressing gown, and all.

"Nothing. I haven't bin up to nothing," he said.

No wife will accept that, especially one who has often received into her home things damaged in transit or fallen from the backs of lorries. This one husband tossed and turned beside her all last night, he'd been snappy this morning. Now he came rushing in with brandy on his breath, the kids in bed, and he is a right old two-and-eight. She said: "Who's coming asking, then?"

"Nobody. Nobody's coming. But if they do, I haven't bin out."

Just the sort of answer to set the bells jangling in any woman who has been secretly fearing for years that her housekeeping money will be reduced suddenly to National Assistance, due to her husband's doing time. No way after that could she be diverted from getting to the bottom of the matter. Not with the kids to think of, the new Georgian bow windows to pay for, the Costa Brava holiday booked, and cold sweat all over the breadwinner's brow. She went to work.

He had known that she would. In his heart he wanted her to. There was love between them, he trusted her. Needed her. Needed now to talk. In a short time she knew it all; except for the drugs. He didn't know himself that some of those hidden trays contained drugs, he thought it was all tobacco. He had no idea that Bert and Clovis were syndicate men, that he, Sydney, was fall guy only, an expendable chosen because known to be bent enough to bite when it was put to him that a doctored vehicle could bring in on selected runs sufficient tobacco, bought at 40p a pack in Amsterdam and sold at £3 here, to supplement very nicely the earnings of a truck driver and his roly-poly new foreman. Who knew already that he was running a bit for himself, in a clumsy amateur way.

"How much you been bringing in, then?" she demanded.

"About a hundred, hundred and fifty pounds at a time."

"What, under the flipping floor? What about the Customs?"

"There's a geezer in Amsterdam, he's bent. I have to use a certain bay, he puts his seal on. I don't do it every trip."

There was indeed a bent geezer in Amsterdam, and he did put his seal on. But he was not interested in tobacco. Nor was he taking any great risk. It is quite impossible, that Customs order demanding the offloading of every great truck and the stripping of it down to the chassis. Never get any business done that way. No real skin off a Customs officer, if a truck with his seal on is looked at later and found to contain contraband. So long as it does not happen too often.

"So who was the geezer you reckon belted you, then?"

"I dunno, do I? It was dark, I didden bleeding see him."

"A copper," she said. "I bet it was a copper. I told you when you brought the washing machine home, you was heading for trouble. I bet they been looking you over. That bloody Bert—I'd like to stick a knife in his guts."

Exactly his own thinking. "For Christ's sake," he said.

"Never mind Christ's sake. What about my sake? What about the kids' sake, if you're going to nick?"

"I *done* it for your sake."

"*I* never asked you to do it for my bleeding sake."

"Ditten mind the Costa Brava, though, did you?" said Sydney. "Ditten mind the bleeding Georgian windows."

Inspector Rosher, at about the time when Superintendent Fisk stirred at the bottom of his stairs and clutched at a bannister to drag himself upright, stepped well back into the shadows. Night-sight had come to him by now, but even so he could not clearly make out all the details. The tubby little feller helping the other along—that was the haulage bloke. The other one—who was that? Couldn't sort him out.

The pub landlord, was it? Feet dragging, one hand held up before him and weirdly dangling. Got pissed in his own pub, had he? Not many landlords do that, not so completely. And if they do, they stay indoors. Don't go walkies, by canals, to be helped home by haulage foremen who just happen to be standing around long after they should have gone home.

But it looked like the pub landlord. And he'd been leaned now against the porch of the pub while the tubby little feller knocked on the door. Cautiously, as it seemed, looking around to spy out anybody watching.

Somebody opened the door. He could not see that it was Mrs. Chafers. But he saw the light shine suddenly forth, revealing that indeed the men were Bert and Mr. Chafers, the latter wiping a hand over the bottom half of his face before using it to prop himself with hanging head against the aged timber upright of the porch. And now the tubby feller moved to support him, one arm round his waist. They passed inside. The door closed.

Inspector Rosher advanced. Came out from the shadows and moved quietly—surprising how quietly he could move, in those boxy-toed shoes—along to the pub. The sensitive antennae of your seasoned policeman come quickly to the twitch.

Here was something funny, happening by night. Anything funny happening by night is matter for twitching over. So: Should he knock on the door? Thunder on it, to shake them? Thunder in when—if—it opened, to confront them, all caught flat-footed?

Tap gently, to be more sure that somebody would answer? Or wait, to see what happened next?

He wished now that his personal radio was not on the blink. What he needed was somebody in support, to watch the back door when he knocked. Without a warrant, he could not legally get inside. But if something bent is afoot, a brisk thunder on a front door often leads to sudden scarpering out through the back.

The hard little eyes in that man's remarkably simian skull missed very little. It is a copper's job to assimilate every detail of the relevant surroundings even as he considers how he should act. Beneath where the landlord had stood with hanging head were small spots on the stone steps.

In the inner breast pocket of the durable blue serge suit, Inspector Rosher carried always a small, flat torch. No policeman working at night is complete without his torch. He brought it out, shone it downward. Blood. The bugger had been bleeding. He lifted the narrow beam. More blood. A patch of it, marking the timber where the bugger had leaned on his hand after wiping it over his face.

So: nothing conclusive. He might have had an accident. Gone for a walk, fallen over, got himself knocked down by a car.

But why Bert?

Well, perhaps he, too, was out for a walk. Or driving the car. Perhaps . . .

Here, Inspector Rosher turned rapidly and rose up onto his toes. Truly, man is a strange little animal. Who would have thought that this bulky one with the black hat low over stern little eyes, rushing suddenly tippy-toe with knees-up action and bum stuck out for the concealment afforded by the side of a pub porch, was a serious policeman, approaching retirement, engaged upon a serious inquiry? But he was, and the door was opening.

Bert emerged. He did not even wish a goodnight on whoever let him out; and once again Rosher, hidden beside the porch, could not see that it was Mrs. Chafers. He could not see Bert, for that matter, until the roly-poly figure hurried clear of the porch, the door closing abruptly behind him. Inspector Rosher took a long stride, saying clearly: "'Evening, Mr.—erum." What was the bugger's name?

The tubby man spun on his axis. "Maa—herha—ha," he said.

"Not drinking after hours, I trust?" The materialized Rosher spoke quite jovially. That terrible joviality. It comes to a copper automatically, when he pops out on somebody up to something.

"Ha. No. No," said Bert.

"Visiting?"

"Er—yeah. Yeah."

"Who was the friend I saw you arrive with?"

"Friend?"

"The one with blood on his face."

"Oh. Yeah. That was—he was the landlord. Mr. Chafers. Yeah."

"Hurt himself, had he?"

"Hurt himself? Oh—yeah."

"How'd he do that?"

Credit must be given again to Bert. It is a terrible, terrible shock when you are up to the ears in bent business all going lopsided, to have a ranking gorilla come looming like that, right out of nowhere on a dark night. But roly-polyness can accumulate round a solid core. His mind was racing with logical thought, even now. It must have been, because he said: "He . . . fell off the boat."

"What boat?" said Rosher. He, too, was thinking, very concisely. But then, he had received no shock.

"His boat. I was—I look after them for him. One's going out tomorrow, needed the starter fixing. I been doing it. That's why I'm here, bit of an emergency. He came to—see me. He tripped up. Fell off the side. Hit his . . . hit himself on the quay."

Nice. Neat. And logical, very plausibly rooted. Bert *did* look after Chafers's boats, he did work on them in the evenings, Chafers might well visit him, bring him a drink, see how work was progressing.

Excellent recovery, really; because Bert's flashing mind must have realized even, that if Rosher was lurking in shadow he could not have had the boats under observation, and wouldn't know if he, Bert, and Chafers, had come from them or from elsewhere.

Rosher knew it for a load of cobblers. He'd watched the scene earlier between this man and Knocker Davis, he'd been there when the little feller bustled into the pub and, seeing him, got out fast. One thing with another: bent. And Chafers in with it. Mrs. Chafers, too?

So: how to proceed? Turn the little man back, knock on the door?

Maybe. But probably they would have fixed the story while Bert was inside. And he, Rosher, could not safely demand ingress. He could request it; they could refuse it. They were not under investigation, and all he had seen was an injured man being helped in. Nothing to do with his murder inquiry. Nothing concrete in it at all. Just this strong whiff of fish in the hairy nostrils and a quivering in the urgent antennae.

No. Let the little bugger carry on. His story could have been true, he could have been working late on emergency fitting out. He said: "Where you going now?"

"Home," said Bert, promptly. "I'm going home."

"Thought you might be rushing off for a doctor. You came out in a hurry."

"Doctor? Oh, no. He don't need no doctor. His missis is fixing him up. It's only a nose-bleed. Made his nose bleed, that's all."

Let him go. And go with him. See him off the premises. Might be interesting to poke about a little after that, in his yard. You never know what you may find once the antennae are itching, and he, the inspector, was going that way. He'd nothing much else to do, really. Nothing but sniff into derelict places, looking for snoring vagrants. "Good. I'll walk along with you," he said.

"Ah," said Bert. "I'm—only going for my car."

"Where'd you leave it?"

"In the yard."

"Suits me. I'm not going anywhere particular."

There was nothing Bert could do about it. Given choice, he would have vanished with no more than a soft plop before the inspector's amazed eyes. His racing brain saw ice, cracking all around. In the pub, the Chafers. And if this bastard held him here, and knocked, would Mrs. Chafers have wit enough to fall in with his story *if* he had a chance to advance it? And how could he have? And Chafers, too dizzy for swift mental capering—he didn't *really* look as if he fell off a boat.

On the whole, better away, in spite of the truck and Clovis's motorscooter still in the yard—and Clovis himself in the warehouse, with the back street door left open, by Christ. He hadn't thought to lock that one, when he came through with all his attention given to manipulating Chafers. "Yeah," he said. "Yeah. Right." He turned, and Rosher fell in beside him. They walked along the quay.

When they came into the yard proper, both sets of eyes scanned it covertly. Nothing obviously fishy, and this was a small relief to Bert, who could not remember whether the back doors of the truck had been closed when he came past, or left ajar by scarpering Sydney, a standing invitation to peer in. They were closed, the vehicle standing huge but innocently out at a distance from the unloading bay. What was more, it hid Clovis's scooter. He had simply abandoned it—with the dope? In the panniers? He should have brought a cardboard box back, but there'd been no chance to think about it. On the far side, but it wasn't hidden, not really. Walk up past the truck and there it would be. The copper was speaking, nodding that hat toward the little glassed-in cubicle.

"That your office?"

"Yeah," said Bert. "Mm."

"Got a phone in there?"

"Yeah."

"Mind if I use it?" Ring Fisk. He ought to be down here, by rights. He, Rosher, was stepping over the edge of his brief. If something extra was looming here, or even if it were related, it was up to Fisk to decide who did what, and to whom. Not that Rosher couldn't, or wouldn't; but there could be cans about if he stepped aside, and Fisk's was the shoulder to which they should be directed. And let this little feller listen, while the call was made. It could be very unsettling for him.

"Yeah," said Bert. "No. It's—er—inside. I'll—er—unlock." Would that fucking motorbike show from there? Walk on.

In the dark of the yard, the scooter remained hidden by the bulk of the truck. Bert switched on the light in his cubicle office and indicated the telephone on the desk. The inspector grunted what might have been thanks, and crossed to pick it up.

He dialed Fisk's number. If the superintendent heard it, he took no notice. It would not have registered properly. When he dragged himself upright and knew she had gone out, he thought to go after her; but you cannot gallop about on a twisted knee and what felt like a broken ankle. He stood a while, shaking his head to clear it while he clung to the bannister for support. Then he hopped through to the living room and to his chair, where he sat down hunched, oblivious to the physical pain and brooding. After a time he hauled himself up and hopped again, to fetch a bottle. He sat now drinking deliberately, dangerously: to dull pain, to stupefy himself, in case he should murder her when she came in.

Rosher listened for some time to the ringing at the other end. Then he broke the connection and dialed again. When the station switchboard replied, he said: "Inspector Rosher here. Is Mr. Fisk there?"

"No," they said. "He's at home."

"I've been trying his home. No answer."

"Well," they said, "that's what it says here. He's at home."

"Uh-huh. Have you taken care of the other matter?"

What other matter? thought Bert, straining his ears toward the reply. All he heard was little dwarfs gabbling.

Constables Wargrave and Kenton were on it, the switchboard was saying. They'd report themselves as having arrived. No sign of subject as yet.

"Right. I want another man down here. He'll find me in the little dead-end street between the warehouses. I'm looking for layabouts. And I want him here now, not in an hour's time. Right?"

Right, they said, resignedly. Every bugger wants everything done now. They pulled out the plug and inserted another.

Rosher hung up, the call having served, he hoped, three purposes. He did need a helper, to watch the pub just in case something happened, and as witness/support should he decide to knock. Also, it took him onto the written-down switchboard record as alive and on the ball while Ernie Fisk was off somewhere, apparently not working. That could not be bad. Also, summoning of another copper must stir up the alarm in this little bugger, if nefarious enterprise were afoot; and little alarmed buggers, stirred sufficiently, often do and say remarkable things. "Right," he said. "Let's go."

"Where to?" said Bert.

"Well, I thought you were going to your car."

"Oh. Yeah, yeah."

"Come on, then. Let's go."

They walked to where cars belonging to the staff were left by day, at the far end of the yard away from the working area. Only Bert's stood here now, and to reach it they passed this side of the truck, so that the scooter remained hidden. Inside the little foreman's head, thought was racing now.

What was he to do? Get in the car, wave goodbye, and scarper? Leave Clovis in the warehouse with the back door open, drugs and smuggled tobacco not even properly concealed in the cellar? More drugs, presumably, with the scooter where this bastard, prowling when he, Bert, had departed, would almost certainly find them?

Or bring out the gun, sheathed in the upholstery under his driver's seat? It needed only the ripping away of the standard canvas lining, he could reach down and do it without stirring from his seat, blow the man away before he knew there was a gun, soon as he got in the car.

But he couldn't do that, he couldn't gun a copper down here. The station knew where he was, so he couldn't be disappeared without trace. Besides, another one was on the way.

Scarper. But—the other syndicate men. Clovis, Peter—one dead—and the fuzz here about that first thing in the morning, if they were not on the way already. The syndicate would not take kindly to his scarpering, leaving the broken reed that Clovis had turned out to be to babble all he knew, when he was picked up.

He had the London number. But how could he ring it, with this bastard sticking close? And if he did, they were not on the spot, they wouldn't know the extent of the problem. They might say eliminate Clovis, they might say blow the copper away. And if he didn't, or couldn't . . . They were ruthless men, especially with this kind of money involved. They could even penetrate the nick to recruit as they recruited him, or to wreak vengeance. Bank account for when he got out to the heavy who would rip a man up, blind him with a jagged bottle. Nasty. And Bert was feeling the loom of the nick.

Then there was Sydney—and the bloody boat was loose, probably being done over even now by the fuzz. And Mulcahy, Chafers . . .

Oh, Christ. All fucked up, all quaking about underfoot. For sure, they'd hold him responsible. Him and Clovis. Sod Clovis.

With the big, apelike bastard standing by, Bert worked his little round belly in behind the wheel, started the engine, leaned forward. His fingers sought and found the loosely fastened section of the canvas cover, left like that when he worked on it for easy ripping in time of need. For a second they hovered. Then he straightened; said good night to the copper and received a grave inclination of the black hat in return; let in his clutch and drove away.

Left standing all alone, Inspector Rosher made note in his little book of the license number. It could be useful at a later date. He never did know he'd been standing so close up to a bullet between those hard little eyes.

11

Constable Wally Wargrave sat beside his good mate and oppo Constable Gordon Kenton in the patrol car parked at the bottom of the street, watching a neat little blue Mini approaching and drawing in toward Mavourneen's house. He said, at just the time when Inspector Rosher set out on his lone sniffing around the yard and wherever else he felt merited a sniff: "That'll be him. Shall we collect him before he goes in?"

"Hang on a tick," said P.C. Kenton. "Might as well let him get inside." Fair enough. Your subject suddenly challenged al fresco has been known to leap over walls, which means chasing him all over people's flowerbeds. He doesn't necessarily, of course. It depends what he's been up to.

"What's he done, anyway?" said P.C. Wargrave.

"Christ knows. You know Old Blubbergut. No details, just fetch him in. What's the bugger's name?"

"Mulcready."

"Right. He's in. Let's go."

It had been a hard day for Brendan Mulcahy. A day not to be taken lightly. Stress was added to it by the fact that from when the office closed he could not stay on the spot, to keep a finger on the pulse. Not without inviting comment. Bert would not have let him, if he'd tried, and he wasn't fool enough to try.

So the day had been horrible, and the evening more so because shot through with uncertainty. He knew nothing of the boat's going adrift, nothing of the Peter incident, nothing of any event taking place after five-thirty. But what he did know was worry enough. The police were about, nosing into Johnnie's death; and the truck was out, all that contraband on board. Coming in this evening, to be offloaded, stuff to be stored under the shop.

He went to Mass, after work. Then, because he did not want to sit at the table facing Mavourneen and her mother, he bought a café meal. He spent the evening at a cinema seeing nothing. And now he came home.

The Widow O'Hara was in bed. Mavourneen waited fully dressed, in the living room. But she did not go out to speak with him. She stayed where she was, keeping the door closed, no light showing under, hearing the front door open, the soft sound of his footsteps ascending the stairs. He'd go to bed. If that Mr. Rosher didn't come back to see him, she'd slip out to telephone, say that he was here.

It startled her, when the policemen set the chime pealing in the silent house. Keyed up as he was, it startled him more. He heard her go to answer—and he'd had no idea she was still up—and her voice at the door, replying to a male rumble. And said to himself at once: Police. Oh, my God. My God.

There was a pause before she tapped on his door, saying softly, "Brendan." But he made no reply, he was pushing the window up. By the time she had waited a second, knocked again, and turned the knob, he was through it. She came in to find just his hands on the sill and a white, wide-eyed face vanishing downward as his feet sought the outhouse roof.

She retreated, called down the stairs: "He's gone out the window."

"We're coming in," cried one of the young policemen. "Where's the back door?"

"Straight through."

P.C.s Wargrave and Kenton went charging through the house, their minds saying in concert—and this is a free transcription—Sod it. Here we go again, all over the bloody flowerbeds.

When Inspector Rosher had watched Bert's rear lights vanish, he tucked his pencil away and went to have a look at the truck. Not with particular intent but because there was nothing else here to look at. All was silent now as the pit dug across jungle paths, into which elephants fall. In the looming shadow behind it he found the scooter, tossed carelessly aside. Not even propped up on its stand. And in the pannier where Clovis had crammed it, the small cardboard box. And in the box, the plastic packages.

No need to ask what this was. He'd come across it before. He prized up a small corner of a flap, shook a little white powder onto the palm of his hand. Heroin, he'd bet on it. And—bloody hell—if it hadn't been let down, if it were high grade, worth Christ knows what, at street prices.

Who dumped it here, then, and left it so carelessly? The little fat feller? Why? Panic?

Who panicked, then? What panicked them? Why?

Don't touch anything more than you have to, there'll be dabs all over the bike even if there's none on the packets.

Where's the back-up I ordered? I need his walkie-talkie. Bloody marvelous, ain't it? You tell 'em straightaway, *now,* and they arrive hours bloody later.

It had not, in fact, been long since Rosher rang the station; and, of course, he should have been carrying his own personal radio, in serviceable order. That's what the regulations say. And the back-up man was here, anyway. A Detective Constable (Jango) Jaggers. Young, but not outrageously. He could, if pressed, have grown a beard.

With commendable good sense, since he was not sure what Old Blubbergut was up to and didn't intend to blow it, he had eschewed the opening of the dead-end street between the warehouses, knowing because he'd done his beat time in this area that he could get in from the haulage-firm yard. So he drove on to the bridge and freewheeled down to the quay, where he left his car. He came on now, up the dark entrance and into the yard. On his way to the gate he met Inspector Rosher, coming out from behind the truck.

"About bloody time," the inspector said. "Let's have your walkie-talkie."

He thrust out a hairy hand. The young man produced his personal radio. The inspector conversed with the station, requesting that somebody be sent from the Drugs Squad to take charge of a cardboard box filled with highly suspect plastic packages. Four more men, two to keep out of sight, eyeing the front of the Ring o' Roses public house; the others similarly tucked away, watching the back. Contact to be made with Mr. Nore-Smith, because his was the ground upon which the goodies were found and he employed the man who surely was deep in. To wit, Bert Humsey. Left five minutes ago in a blue Jag, license number (out with the book) HXJ 108 V. Put an EMTAD out for him—get him in. Anything heard of Mr. Fisk?

Scribbling busily, they said no. Nothing. An EMTAD, for those who care, is an Emergency Message to All Districts. It covers the country.

''Have you tried to locate him?''

''Well, no,'' they said. ''We didn't know he was wanted.''

''Try him on the blower. If you can't raise him, send somebody up.'' No time for covering, this, no time for pussy-footing. There were cans about, and Fisk was on duty. If they found him pissed and passed out, too bad for him, he should have confined it to his leisure time. Too many rabbit holes here for one ferret alone.

''Right,'' they said. ''Right—we'll do that.'' And they would, with alacrity. They, too, were ever alert for cans suddenly zooming, and they were wondering if perhaps they should have done it before, at the time of Old Blubbergut's earlier call.

''Don't have the lads drive down to the quay,'' the inspector said, ''they'll be seen from the pub. They can get into a narrow street between the warehouses. There's a gate at the end, lets into the haulage-firm yard. I'll be waiting for them.''

Bloody hell, thought Constable Jaggers. I drove down onto the quay, my car's there now. Well, I didn't know, did I?

''Right,'' they said. Almost before connection was severed, they were busy: rousing out the Drugs Squad, getting the four men away, diverting a squad car from its beat, telling it to call at Superintendent Fisk's house, seeing that everything was all right. It arrived, this car, soon after Fisk let fly a bottle at his wife. It got her smack on the temple, and she dropped like a stone.

Inspector Rosher handed back the young man's personal radio. He said: ''Right, lad. First off, we're going to have a look inside that truck. Then—'' he broke off because Clovis had come through the gate, acting weird. Here is the reason:

Left alone in the shop, shattered not so much by fear as by shock and sheer horror at the sudden conversion of his warm beloved into a rag dolly lying among strange legs on the charity-chill stone of a canal lock, he needed a fix as never before. Even commonsense—such residue of it as remained—said he needed a fix. There were other things to be thought about: helmets left on the boat and the like. He couldn't think in this condition, he must break the stone wall of horror. And grass wouldn't do it. He'd rolled and smoked as soon as Bert left.

Well, he knew where the junk was. They were stowing it in the cellar.

Among fraternities of homosexuals, artists, musicians, writers, students, et al, the use of grass is almost de rigueur. Even the big, very cautious drug syndicates permit it among their proven personnel, looking upon it as harmless. But they clout very heavily if the subject moves on to the hard stuff, especially if he starts dipping into the stocks. Oh, it is known, the stuff is there, and not even the destruction of the pitiful street buyer takes place before the eyes of he who moves in between entry into the country and your actual distributors. But those who succumb are invariably found in the end lying in a wood with a hole in the head or floating face down somewhere. If they are found at all.

So Clovis, although he had been a syndicate man from way back to when he abandoned ballet for this more lucrative field, had never known the hard stuff after an experimental sniff or two, the effects of which had not been all that exciting. Restored—at least, slightly elevated—by the joint he had smoked already, he crept down to the cellar (no problem in quitting the shop, he used the other door), where he found by the light of a match the trays holding tobacco and that other one; from which he took a packet, shook out a little of the white powder, and sniffed. Snuffed up much more than he should have done, with marijuana already aboard. Didn't fully realize—he certainly was not thinking clearly—the effect it would have.

It did clarify his thinking, for a little space. Long enough for him to remember the scooter, and what he had left with it. So: he'd go and get it. Euphoria was taking him over, he was CLOVIS, he had nothing to fear from any man.

He was clear of the building when the need to dance came upon him. He saw no reason to deny himself. By the time he reached the gate, he was flying along, high above the earth in a golden, pulsating sun-glow. And he'd forgotten completely what he was coming for.

Nevertheless, he came through the gate and whirled, arms extending gracefully as he kicked it shut behind him. He then danced on, not toward the truck behind which he had left his scooter but toward the exit onto the quay; which caused Inspector Rosher to terminate unfinished his instructions to Constable (Jango) Jaggers and stand with his mental jaw dropped. This did not show on the skin-surface, which merely shifted into a scowl. It normally did, given surprising matter to contemplate. Young Jango Jaggers said softly: ''What the heck's he up to?''

The inspector shoved the cardboard box upon him. ''Get hold of this,'' he commanded. ''Stay here with it.'' And he moved off, following in the wake of Clovis as that man went footing light and fantastic across the yard. Rosher would have needed a gallop to keep him in touch, but for the fact that he retarded onward progress frequently by running tiptoe round in a wide circle, fluid hands dealing peculiar caresses to whoever he believed stood about the perimeter. Chorus dancers, presumably, all posed up and available. Or little male angels. Or even big, bare-bummed Hottentots. Or he may just have been touching up the pretty flowers. Who knows what the hopped-up are seeing?

An experienced policeman when he knows he is about to finger a collar does not go flying bald-headed at it. Rosher was in no hurry, he was going to have the geezer—the pouf, that's who it was. But not here, where he had space to break aside, necessitating chasing and sweat expended. Let him get into the exit alley, where he could be pinned. Take it easy, don't panic him into flight. He might be mad, he might be Brahms-and-Liszt, he might be hopped-up. Each of these conditions, or any permutation, means unpredictable. Easy, easy.

The young policeman left behind, clutching his cardboard box, watched his superior stalking the dipping, skittering subject like a sheepdog subtly penning a flighty ewe, until they disappeared into the darker alley. He said to himself: Never a dull moment, is there? Well, it's better than working for the Co-op. Four years he wasted with the Co-op, before he joined the force. He might, they said plaintively when he left, have risen in time to branch manager. But he turned his back on all that glory.

Rosher spoke for the first time when he had the subject committed to the exit passage, or to a quick belt with the Hammer if he came this way, trying to backtrack. He said, jovially: ''Hello, my son. Dancing, are we?''

Subject did not answer, and he did come this way. His face rapt and ecstatic, he wheeled and came sweetly with fingers fluttering, languid arms wafting like the wings of the dying swan he may at this moment have been. Rosher folded his awesome fist, feeling the muscles bunch in his shoulder as he cocked it.

Rarely, very, very rarely, was he taken by surprise in a situation involving potential action, especially when he stood balanced on the balls of his feet with the safety catch off. How often does Clint Eastwood fall with a bullet in the belly? But Clovis managed it. Clovis took him by surprise.

He never actually came within range. He fluttered on; and just as the Mighty Hammer moved back six inches, he went into the air to deliver the same pointed foot that broke that poor man's teeth, back there on the towpath. He was wearing heavy biking boots, remember.

Yes, there is no gainsaying it. Inspector Rosher was taken by surprise. His mental approach was, of course, all wrong. He believed, with contempt—it is a common error—that to be queer is to be cream-puff. Aye, but a queer ballet dancer is, in fact, a highly trained and solidly muscular athlete. Think it out for yourself. Clovis had slipped a bit; but much of the swift agility lingers, all the way to old age. Rosher never tangled with a ballet dancer before.

Justice, then. Had he known better, had he considered the opposition as man, the Hammer would have been in before the foot. As it is, he did manage to roll somewhat with the punch. The flashing boot took him on the side of the jaw, staggering him against the wall and dazing him momentarily. Light flashed behind his eyes, but the hat remained steady. Clovis twirled, and danced on.

By fighter's instinct Rosher came off that wall as he came off the ropes, similarly belted in his boxing days; crouched low with guard up, braced on the flats of his feet. But even this delay gave Clovis a three-, four-yard start on his way down to the quay, and the canal.

Rosher started after him. Not cautiously now but charging, with blood up. A bad man to tangle with if you did not fell him thoroughly at the first blow. To put pain into his jaw, to daze him was not enough. It merely stripped away the surface veneer, paring him down to what he basically was: the elemental fighting man, now with lips drawn back and snarling.

He was closing on Clovis when they came out onto the quay, where the man danced straight on, to the stone-slab edge of the canal. Whether he knew who or even what Rosher was is doubtful, in his condition. But presumably he knew somebody or something was closing with him, because still with the ecstatic look on his face he whirled here, and tried his leaping, flashing kick again.

You do not catch a Rosher twice with the same flash trick. And this one, when you know the man may do it, is easily dealt with, almost the A in the alphabet of unarmed combat. Down went the inspector's head, his linked hands sweeping upward hit Clovis hard, just above the airborne ankle. Clovis, already in the air, went somersaulting backward in a sudden flailing angularity of arms and legs, to vanish with an almighty splosh into the canal.

Almost, the inspector followed him in. There are dog whistles indiscernable to the human ear. So might there have been a skreek, a tinge about of burning compo from the soles of his boxy-toed shoes as he braked, teetering on the edge, waving his arms to aid balance and snarling aloud: "How about that, you bastard?" as he waited for subject to surface.

Clovis came up almost immediately, but he made no attempt to swim, or even to stay afloat. Beaming beatifically he bobbed up, head and shoulders, and happily sank again.

Drown, you sod, drown, blazed Rosher's still blood-lusty rage; and he even looked around to make sure nobody was watching. He'd have left the bastard there, all right. His mind was already composing: He got away—must have fallen in while I was looking for him. By the time I found him, there was nothing to do but wring him out.

But then he thought, as happy Clovis bobbed up again, the lad up in the yard. He won't swallow that, I'd have called him. And he'd know I must have heard the splash.

And now the sane part of him spoke, the professional part. Don't be daft, fish him out. A nutter, that's all he is. Besides, he's part of the general oddity down here. Must be. We need him. It's all coming together—he's been sampling the stock. Then he thought: Sod it. And pausing only to peel off his shoes and the jacket of his durable blue serge suit (not the trousers; other people might arrive, and a foolish figure of fun is the copper in saturated shirttails) and to place the black hat carefully on top of it, he leaped into the canal. Sanity returned, duty and humanity both mitigated against letting the bugger drown. But he proceeded savagely. Who needs to leap into a canal by night, clad in his shirt and trousers? Given time, he'd have sent the young Jango Jaggers.

The water felt quite warm. It usually does, when you enter it with September night-nip in the air. No problem finding Clovis, he surfaced again a yard or two away, still beatific, still making no effort at self-salvation. Rosher had him by the collar in no time. And now he galvanized, flailing his arms and struggling. Fighting? Or merely trying, belatedly, to save himself?

The point is academic. Down swept the Hammer, ungalvanizing him completely. A fair tow for Rosher, getting him right along to the steps leading up to the cobblestones, near where the boats were moored.

When she stepped over her husband and swept raging out of the house, Mrs. Fisk had been headed for the club where a man waited. A few drinks, a trip to his flat—a pleasant evening. Clothes back on, and home in her little red motorcar. She'd done it before, often enough; but never before had she left the husband lying huddled at the foot of the stairs.

The same diminution of red rage that enabled Rosher to see that he would do better not to let Clovis drown came to her before she reached the club. She drew in to the curb, switched off the engine, and sat for some time.

Suppose he were dead? Or at least badly injured—carpet or not, a fall like that can break a neck. Or a back.

Benefit of the doubt to her. Nobody is all bad, and when she turned the ignition key and drove to where she could turn to drive back the way she had come, she may well have been motivated by concern for him. By guilt, at the very least.

On the other hand, she may have done it because if there does happen to be a corpse lying about the house, inviting all sorts of awkward questions, it being a high-ranking policeman, it must be better to report it the acceptable side of midnight rather than at two in the morning.

Another thought: If he were merely injured—had to be removed to hospital, say—better be the one who rings for the ambulance soon after the event, present with her own story, than the one who rolls home after gadding, all dolled up in gadding dress, to find him gone and his police waiting, he having said she pushed him down the stairs. The evening was ruined, anyway. She'd be wondering all the time what was happening back there.

People leaving houses in a blind rage do not pause to click switches, so she came into a lit hall. He was not where she had left him. He must be all right, he must be alive and able to walk. She'd been scaring herself unnecessarily, probably he'd only bumped his head. Or passed out for a little while, the drunken sot. Perhaps, having checked, she could set off again.

The living room light, also, was on. She did not need to guess where he would be; the drinks were in there. She walked through, to find him hunched in his chair, unfocusable eyes glaring at her, bottle poised above the glass. Drawing herself stiffly upright, she snapped: "Well?"

He made no verbal answer. For a second he glared; and then with a powerful twist he hurled the bottle at her. One flash of white light and she went down like a stone. Never felt a thing.

His liquor-dizzy eyes widened for a moment and he moved his injured leg, making as if to rise. Then he dropped the glass and his hands went up to cover his face. He sat weeping, weakly, drunkenly. And then he passed out, sagging backward in his chair with his face pointed to the ceiling that he'd papered in blue and with a pattern of little stars, to please his other wife.

The police arrived soon after. Two young constables, diverted in their patrol car. One was blue-eyed, the other was balding. They rang the bell, they knocked on the door, and they got no answer. The blue-eyed one said: "What do we do now?"

"Look around," said the balding one. They had no firm instruction as to how they should proceed, but it seemed the obvious thing to do.

When policemen inspect a house, sooner or later they wind up at the back. These two, when they got there, found the living room light on, shining through the curtained french window into the garden. "Think he's in there?" the blue-eyed young man said.

"Tap on the glass," advised his oppo.

The constable did so; and nobody broke the silence. He tried the handle. It was unfastened. He said: "Could he do us for illegal entry?" and opened the window, pushing aside the curtain to peer in. Then he said: "Christ!"

The balding man had looked in over his shoulder. Already he was producing his personal radio, pulling out the little aerial. His oppo said:

"Not . . . dead. Are they?"

When Bert Humsey drove away, leaving Inspector Rosher standing in the yard amid all those goodies and Clovis and the rest of it, his mind leaped wildly up and down and all around the situation, finding nothing to cheer about. He was, in his way, a man of courage; had he not been, the syndicate would never have trusted him as active organizer (uncourageous Clovis was trusted only with the overall brainwork, and as paymaster), and not prone to panic. But he badly needed support now. He didn't know what to do. Instinct said scarper. Self-disciplined habit said no, not yet. Chicken out now, *everything's* buggered. *You're* buggered. For life. And you'll never know how long that's going to last.

Another thing (he thought): Where are you going to go? Overseas? You haven't got any money, can't get at it right now, just like that. And if that bloody gorilla's sent the balloon up, they'll be watching for you, airports, ferry ports, and everywhere. And you'll need clothes—you can't go in overalls—and your passport's there, so you'll have to go home. And they'll be watching that, too.

Truly, it was a bloody mess, and all churned up so quickly. He should, he thought now, have blown the bastard away. Another was coming in, yes; but there'd have been some sort of chance to bundle the gear out of it, and Clovis too. And only the bastard had seen him going into the pub with Chafers and coming out after. Now, it was too late. Besides, they carry little radios; he might have been talking to the station while he lurked in the shadows. You just don't know. His call from the office might just have been a little extra. It seemed a bit funny, his needing to make it at all.

Seeking some loophole, some chink through which he could scramble, some course of action that would—or even might—redeem the situation, he kept driving with no real destination in view. He had a flat; but on the ground floor lived his landlady, and she would know he was in, if—when—the fuzz called. His car outside would tell them, anyway. He couldn't hide out there. Besides, it was only a few minutes away from the yard, at a moderate walk, and the shaken criminal mind does not relish lingering on the very brink of the upsetting action. As soon as the gear was found, the bastards would be round in a wink. The bloody gorilla could trot there himself, soon as he knew the address. And it wouldn't take long to find that out. Plus the details of his previous form.

He was through the town and turning onto the bypass when he saw a telephone booth, set conveniently in a layby. He did need to spread the load, he did need some sort of power behind him. It couldn't make his situation worse, to ring London. They'd know soon enough that it was all up the stick, anyway. At least he could warn them, give them a chance to cover tracks. His tracks? Maybe even that. He didn't really know how they responded when things went wrong. But they were hard men and, for sure, they'd mark him down if he let it all happen without telling them.

Yes—he'd ring London. Had the number in his wallet. Knew it by heart, anyway, he'd rung it often enough before. And always most courteously received.

Ringing London or anywhere else from a callbox a long way away is difficult. You must fumble for tenpenny pieces. He had only one. It would do—he'd give the booth number and they could ring him back. He didn't like it, standing here totally exposed, but it was the only thing he could do.

He dialed, and stood with the instrument to his ear, his eyes ranging up and down the long, wide road. Cars about, but nothing to bring the heart into his mouth. When the sudden staccato bip-bip-bip said that connection was made, he sent his tenpenny piece thunking into the box, and a mellifluous feminine voice said, most soothingly: "Mr. Sefton-Jonas regrets that he is not available. If you will leave your number, he will ring you back as soon as he comes in. Burp. Chonk. Mr. Sefton-Jonas regrets he is not available. If you . . ."

Bert hung up. "Fuck it," he said. And when he got back to his car, another thought came to him: He couldn't go to anywhere more than about thirty miles away. He was low on petrol, and the little money in his pocket would hardly run to a gallon, at today's prices.

He'd *have* to go home. Or pinch another car, and that's dicey, for one not used to doing it. Besides, how do you insure against grabbing one with even less in the tank?

No, he couldn't risk prowling about this late in a town area, trying the handles of parked cars. Opening them up, using a bit of wire to start them—what wire? he hadn't got any wire—was a matter for pros, or herberts looking for a joyride.

At home was petrol money enough. And checkbooks, his passport, his credit cards, to gain him plane tickets, ferry tickets, and decent clothes. Given these, he stood some sort of chance. Get to the Continent, even the syndicate wouldn't know where he was. For a while. Long enough, perhaps, for him to strip out the Swiss bank accounts. He'd have to leave the one in Holland; but he'd have plenty to keep him happy for a long, long while. In South America? Maybe. If Ronnie Biggs could do it . . .

So he turned for home, driving swiftly now. Just a quick dash in and out, that's all he needed. Grab what money was there—a decent suit, a shirt, a tie, shoes, documents. And away. Keep a sharp eye out for fuzz, that's all.

He couldn't know it, but this far he was safer than he thought. The police did not as yet have his home address. He had been resident for too short a time to appear on electoral rolls, and when they rang Mr. Nore-Smith, the maid said he was out, at a business function in the big city. They tried to contact him there, but he had gone on with a party to a club. Nobody knew which, or where. Now policemen were calling at every club in the city area.

No Old Bill about, then, when Bert slipped in and out again in under two minutes. He did not linger to pack a suitcase. Slung the necessary clothes over his arm, shoved passport, checkbook, bank documents—he would need them to clear the overseas accounts—and credit cards into the capacious pocket of his overalls, and was gone. Didn't even see his landlady, who was watching a late movie on television and drinking a glass of stout. She took it for medicinal purposes, although, as she said, it made her heave.

He dumped the clothes on the passenger seat beside him and took off. There would be a layby somewhere, a quiet picnic area in the country maybe, where he could change. Get away from here, that was the thing. And fill right up with petrol at the first late night filling station. So take the main road again. No late-serving garages in the lanes.

His one mistake he made when he reached the first garage still open for business. The forecourt was hidden on his approach side by buildings, and it was not until he was turning in and committed to entering that he saw two policemen here, standing by their car and speaking with a man who might have been the night staff, taker of money and manipulator of the pumps.

He was, in fact, the night man; and these were two perfectly innocent policemen who called in every night about this time, they or whatever colleagues were doing graveyard shift, for a chat and a quick cupper, maybe a drag on a cigarette if they had time. It whiles away ten minutes; and God, the night stint needs whiling.

He should have gone boldly forward, of course. They were leaving anyway, they would undoubtedly have cut short the farewell chat and driven away so that the man could attend to this arriving customer. But Bert had no way of knowing it, and policemen were looming in his mind as something to stay away from. This sudden proximity panicked him for a moment. In that little moment, he made his mistake.

He tried to drive out. Swung the wheel to make a U-turn back through the entrance and knew at once that to persevere would mean hitting the low wall separating garage from road. So he swung back, which caused the car to lurch. And then drove on, past the pumps, out at the far entrance, and onto the road again. The two policemen felt a lift at the heart. Here was a little something. This time of night, probably a green-crystal job, trying to avoid them. "Let's have a look at him, eh?" said one, and they slammed themselves into their car.

They saw at once that they were onto something because he was traveling fast, and when he knew they were coming after him, he went faster yet.

Now police drivers love this. Let's face it, this is what they are trained for, they keep their vehicles tuned for it. Car and driver both hate poodling through an eight-hour patrol at respectable speeds. Both come whooping into their kingdom when the foot goes down.

A Jag well driven can outpace most things on a thinly trafficked open road, but not a well-tuned police car. This one clung, siren screaming. Gaining nothing, it's true, but losing nothing either, over hill, over dale, and on toward the big city. And for the latter part of the trip, the policemen knew who they were chasing. The passenger one had his binoculars to his eyes when he said: "Know something, Charlie? That numberplate's the one they gave us on the EMTAD."

"Oh, goodie-good," said his oppo. "Better get on the radio, then, eh?"

The passenger used his mike; so cars were converging on Bert as he raced cityward. And they didn't have to do a thing, after all that fuss and hurry.

He ran out of gas. That's all. Under his foot the engine stuttered, and stuttered, and died. He coasted to a halt at the roadside. What else could he do? Even the vibrant, thrusting, butch-muscled Jag is suddenly no more than an immobile heap of embarrassing metal when it runs out of gas.

He had fumbled under his seat by the time the police car drew in, but he left the canvas unripped, the gun where it was. He was not by nature a killer, and not stupid enough to act blindly for long. What are you going to do, then? his mind asked him dully as they left their car and approached. Murder two of 'em? Coppers? Nick their car? Because yours won't work? Don't be daft—how far do you think you'd get? How *long* do you think you'd get? Thirty years? And here comes another of 'em.

He removed his hand from down by his feet as a second police car screamed in and the two men from the first came up. Warily, although it did not show in them. No copper knows these days what will happen when a man is stopped, subject of an EMTAD. One signaled, telling him to wind the window down; and when he did, spoke quite pleasantly.

"Good evening, sir. Mr. Albert Romsey?"

"Humsey," said Bert. "Albert Humsey."

You cannot always hear too clearly, through all that static. "Would you mind getting out of your car, sir?" the policeman said.

And there was Bert. Done for, ignominiously. But not so ignominiously as young Brendan Mulcahy. Not even a chase over the flowerbeds for him, he never got out of the garden. They found him trying to hide behind one of those dwarfish and starveling shrubs which seem to be all the Irish can manage in a garden once they leave that blessed island where, in pockets on the lower slopes of the Knockmealdown Mountains, the soil is so rich that a seed dropped between the feet explodes with such force and fury as to hit you right in the crotch, should you fail to leap backward pretty sharpish.

12

Inspector Rosher bunched his hairy knuckles to rap upon the Chief Constable's office door the next morning a little later than he should have done. Nobody would bang him for this, he had been up all night and working, after a trip to the hospital for checking and drying out. Clovis needed an ambulance because it had been necessary to belt him once or twice, to quieten him; so the inspector went along. He himself had to be checked and dried, if only for official records, otherwise he would not have bothered. He'd survived without disintegration far worse things than a sudden dip by night in a canal.

The Chief Constable certainly would not be banging. He it was, called from his bed by the uprush of events, who commanded after dawn that Rosher take a few hours off, get a bit of rest, a shave, a meal. Go home, feed his budgie, take a bath, read Kipling, prune a rose, do whatever he liked. But take a few hours off.

Rosher did some of these things; but he had no budgie, he never read if he could help it, and the roses, unpruned since his fat wife went home weeping to Mother, stood now like small apple trees, with late blooms all up at the top. He did not need a bath, they had dunked him at the hospital; but he shaved, fried himself a meal, pushed the vacuum cleaner around, and dozed a while in his chair before setting out again. The only reason he was late: traffic jam, caused by a baker's van and a bus colliding in the town center.

The Chief Constable himself had been hectically engaged since the small hours. On top of the sudden influx of arrestees and general kerfuffle sparked off by Rosher had come the Fisk business, necessitating a trip to the hospital and the need to sort out a replacement to head the inquiry into the murder of John Patrick O'Hara. Mr. Fisk was out of the hunt.

So among those heads of involved departments taking coffee at the chief's morning conference when Rosher came in was Chief

Superintendent (Percy) Fillimore, narrow-skulled and sipping delicately between narrow little snaps at a Garibaldi biscuit. Here not because the chief wished it—that man knew only too well the chalk-and-cheese antipolarity between Fillimore and Rosher—but simply because he was the only available CID officer of sufficient rank to be acceptable to the Home Office as leader of a murder team. God knows, the chief faced enough problems without inviting more. He'd have to explain in officialese what had happened to Chief Superintendent Fisk—who should not, they would probably say, have been appointed if his problem was known in the first place. Even a chief constable can find himself ducking under the whizzing rocket. The Home Office has a very beady eye.

But the chief was not too worried. He had what looked like a major drug case flushed up by one of his inspectors, and the apparent perpetrators locked up nicely, one of them arrested by that same inspector. Wherefore he beamed upon that inspector as he came in and said: "Ah, Mr. Rosher. Up and at it again, I see."

"Sorry I'm late, sir," the inspector said.

"Not at all, not at all. No worse for your—er—dip, I trust?"

"No, sir." As a matter of fact, Rosher looked rather sharper than usual. When the hospital laundry dried his suit, they put it under the steam presser. Knife-edge creases they gave him, not only to the trousers but right up the arms of the durable blue serge jacket. And the jacket wasn't even wet. Good job they didn't get at the hat.

"Good. Splendid. Coffee?"

"No, thank you, sir." A hasty answer. Most policemen hate delicate china, and up here coffee came in fragile little cups, such as tend to disintegrate in the grip of hairy fingers. Also, there was the need to concentrate upon eliminating sucking-up noises. Rosher was not the only man who deplored the chief's benign custom of coffee with the morning conference.

"Help yourself to biscuits. Excellent work last night. Splendid."

"Thank you, sir." Kudos. Public kudos. And Percy's eyes glinting over the rim of his daft little cup, Percy's lips compressed into a narrow thin line when the cup went down. Handled bone china well, Percy did. Had a wife who had trained him to it, and the necessary long, bony digits.

"We were just reviewing the situation." The chief, in fact, had been doing the reviewing. It was his usual practice. The other men sat imbibing coffee. He resumed now, probably recapping a little for the newcomer's sake. Two crash helmets stood on his desk. He picked them up one after the other, and peered into the interiors as he spoke.

"There can be no doubt that the *Happy Lady* boat was being used to transport drugs. Our fellows—" he nodded to the burly and reprehensively scruffy head of the Drugs Squad, who gravely inclined his tatty head; looked as if he normally took his coffee out of a discarded soup can—"have been over it, found a compartment apparently constructed especially. The two men Henderson and—er—Peter Briggins were surprised on board, apparently trying to steal or recover the consignment obviously hidden there. In their panic they left behind two helmets, clearly marked with their names. The lad Briggins fell into the lock and was killed, body in the mortuary. Two packets of drugs in his possession, recovered and now with Superintendent Quigley." The scruff inclined his head again. The chief spoke on.

"The other man was later arrested by Inspector Rosher, who also recovered what appears to be the rest of the cargo from the boat. Admirable piece of work. Splendid. I am sure we all congratulate him."

Everybody murmured. Except Percy, who glinted again.

"So we now have the boat proprietor and his wife downstairs, the man having suffered quite severe facial injury. Nothing to do with us, his wife was attending to him when we arrived. Again, thanks to Mr. Rosher, who directed that they be brought in for questioning before he departed for the hospital. Admirable command of the situation, considering his own condition at the time."

A warm smile, beamed straight at the inspector. Oh, but our man was riding high.

"We also have downstairs the man Brendan Mulcahy, apparently connected to the case in some way, and the transport foreman Herbert George Humsey, in whose car was found a .44 automatic pistol when the vehicle was searched after his arrest. Again thanks to Mr. Rosher, who supplied description of the car and registration number, thus facilitating early identification.''

Higher and higher, Rosher was going. More and more glinty was Percy. Even some of the other men were beginning to look embarrassed. One or two coughed. Damn it, a copper's job is to facilitate arrest. No need to keep on about it.

Distraction came. The interior telephone rang. The chief put down Clovis's helmet and clicked his little switch. Put the receiver to his ear and said: ''Yes? Uh-huh. Mm. Ah. Splendid. Good. Good. Uh-huh. Thank you.'' He then replaced the instrument and addressed the assembled company.

''Wider still and wider. A Mr. and Mrs. Kelly down with Reception, wanting to speak with somebody. He is, he says, driver of the truck found with its flooring dismantled in the Nore-Smith yard last night.''

Poor Sydney. Awful night he'd had, what with the wife and everything. She it was, really, who brought him in. By this morning, he was quite unable to act for himself. The early news bulletin—they battled it out against a background of Radio One—mentioned the arrests and the police belief that drugs were involved. So here he was, squatting on a hard bench under the *Have You Seen This Man?* posters showing subhumans who would have been arrested instantly if they walked about looking like that, with his wife clinging to his arm. If ever a couple looked cold, starved, and miserable.

''You will deal with that, of course, Mr. Quigley.'' Again, the Drugs Squad chief inclined hair that surely was dressed daily with rancid mutton fat. They have very funny habits, Drugs Squad men. ''Good. No doubt he can tell you who is involved on the other side of the Channel. And perhaps where the boat was delivering to.''

''We think we know that,'' the drugs man said in a surprisingly cultured and mellifluous voice. ''Benham's yard in the city, we think. I've got lads there now. Interviewing a Benjamin Johnson.

Form for peddling, form for possession. Seems a fair bet.''

''Excellent,'' said the chief. ''Might have it all nicely cleared by the time these Scotland Yard men arrive, eh?''

''We'll try, sir.'' the drugs man said. And he would. Smaller policemen, if they can feather their caps by having done the chicken-plucking before the Special Branch arrives—as it must, if a drugs case is clearly major, with international connection—chuckle happily all the way to retirement, and die with upturned lips. They do not like Scotland Yard.

''Well,'' said the chief. ''That seems to be working out splendidly. Your man is still at the hospital, Mr. Rosher. Still affected by the overdose, but he's in no danger. He should be with us later in the day.'' The warm beam embraced them all. ''Getting quite crowded in the basement, are we not? More coffee, anyone? No? Well, perhaps we should—er—'' Signal that the session was over. Back to work, chop chop. As his minions supped up and rose hurriedly, those who had found seats, the chief added: ''None of this, of course, advances our murder inquiry. If you will spare me a minute, Mr. Fillimore, Mr. Rosher?''

When the other men had filed out, the chief spoke again, addressing the inspector, who stood burly and knife-edged just inside the door, where he had stayed after he came in. ''Mr.—er—Fisk will be relinquishing the case, Mr. Rosher.''

''Uh-huh,'' said Rosher, face impassive as King Kong's death mask. ''How is—er—Mr. Fisk?''

''Not too good, I'm afraid.'' In hospital. Complete collapse—acute alcoholic poisoning (he really caned that last bottle). Lucky to be alive, they said, he could have choked on vomit had those two policemen not arrived. If a copper can be said to be lucky, who lives to face a career in ruins and criminal charges too grave to be swept under any mat. All this on top of the pain that led him to it.

''Uh-huh. And Mrs. Fisk?''

''She will—er—be all right.'' *Should* be all right, the hospital said. The bottle, fortunately, just missed the killing point of the temple proper; but who can tell, they said, what a blow like that will do? She won't die, they said; but we can't estimate the effect upon the brain until she comes round.

So Superintendent Fisk faced, at the very least, charges of assault causing actual physical damage. Marginally better, perhaps, than if his aim had been a fraction to the right. That would have been murder? Manslaughter, more likely. In any case, there went Fisk; and the chief brushed the matter aside. Not callously, but because what more could a man in his position say, to men in their position? Again he addressed Rosher.

"Mr. Fillimore will be taking the inquiry over. You will, of course, work with him as—er—harmoniously as—er. You will, of course, acquaint him with whatever progress has—er—come your way."

The narrow eyes glittered in the narrow skull of Chief Superintendent Fillimore as he fastened them on the inspector, harsh and unyielding. Rosher's gorillalike impassivity took on sternness, his own little eyes hard as jet beads. "Mm," he said. "Rrmph." He drew out his great gray handkerchief.

When the echoes died away, the chief relinquished his white-knuckled grip on the edge of his beautiful desk and said while the dust motes still danced in the air: "All right, gentlemen. Thank you. That will be all."

13

When Inspector Rosher walked all covered in roses out of the Chief Constable's office, to all intent and purpose he walked right off the drugs case. He must produce a written report, of course, he would give evidence in court, he might be called upon to verify or clarify the odd point between now and then. But the Drugs Squad must take over now, working with the Special Branch men when they arrived from Scotland Yard. And very happy these specialized local men were.

Why would they not be? Here was a gift from a God who hands out such neatly wrapped packages so rarely it is not always clear whose side He is on. Long before the chief's meeting they had fallen upon it enthusiastically, probing, working to demolish those in the cells downstairs, preferably before the men from the Smoke got here.

Oh, it was big all right. No drugs caper functions in isolation. There would be connection in London, in Amsterdam, right back along a chain to the Middle East, to South America, to the States. Somebody produces the stuff, somebody refines it, somebody smuggles it out, somebody smuggles it in—and somebody flogs it. A big operation, inevitably involving a lot of people. Everything on a much grander scale than the little men linked on at the end of the chain may realize.

Every so often, in any profession, comes one of those days that makes the whole thing seem almost worthwhile. For the local Drug Squad, this was one. Birdies were singing, and they glowed as they listened to the music. Didn't let it show, of course. Kept their eyes very stern, their faces iron-hard.

It was the amateurs who sang. The one true professional, Herbert George Humsey, was saying nothing. They wept no tears over that. The testimony of others would do for him, and others were more than willing to testify.

Edwin Chafers, for one. His wife, who hated him, was snarling like a wildcat and trying to shift all the sin onto him. He, obsequious and obstreperous by turn and speaking out of an empurpled, swollen face, blamed Bert, who had enticed him into allowing his boat to be used for the delivery of smuggled tobacco to a point somewhere on the normal cruising run. No, he didn't know where. Added pale green to purple when told no trace of tobacco was found on board. Only drugs. Swore frantically that he knew nothing at all about it. "I'm innocent! Innocent, I tell you—innocent!"

Well, he's no problem, the interrogating officers told each other when they left him alone to think. Give him an hour, he'll be offering to turn state's evidence. Of course they were right. They know their business.

Then there was young Brendan Mulcahy, singing already before the two arresting policemen got him to the station, even. It was Bert. Bert, when he himself was working for another haulage firm in Amsterdam.

Oh yes, he admitted he came here from Amsterdam, they hardly needed to produce his passport. Bert, come over ostensibly to deal with a recalcitrant truck, sought him out and took him for a meal. Seemed to know he was engaged already in small-scale tobacco smuggling—many drivers run a little bit in from the Continent, in collusion with a man on the spot who has contacts—and suggested that if he, Bert, could fix him a job as checker for Nore-Smith's at the receiving end, the game could be very lucratively enlarged. Three-way split between himself, Bert, and the driver already doing a bit, and ready to do more.

That's all he knew. He fixed the Amsterdam end, came over when Bert whistled, and started work. Checked everything off without question, including boxes from under the floor, or packed, when there was overflow, in the washing machine cartons, to be codemarked and stood aside until removed and stashed privily.

No, he said, he didn't know how Bert distributed it from there. By car, he thought, in one lot, to a collusive wholesale tobacconist somewhere. All he did was check, and pocket the money. He, too, took on a green sheen over his gray pallor when drugs were mentioned. No, no—not drugs. He didn't know anything about drugs, or boats, or the Chafers, or the queers in the shop. Tobacco. Only tobacco. He swore it by the Sacred Heart of Jesus.

The police were inclined to believe him. Whether the judge would was quite another matter. Crafty bugger, this Humsey, they told each other as they walked away. Latched onto the existing caper, buried the big stuff in with the little stuff. Used the little men, kept 'em in the dark about the big thing. Let's have a word with this driver.

Poor Sydney. They got no more from him than they did from Mulcahy. He brought tobacco in. Bert—it was Bert. Bert rigged the truck, Bert told him which Customs lane he must use, in Holland and over here. He didn't even load it, it was slipped aboard by a bloke in Holland.

Yes, he knew where it went to, sometimes he took it himself. Fogen, wholesale tobacconist in the big city, he'd known him for years. There was a lot of green, glistening skin about today. It came on people as soon as drugs were introduced into a conversation. "Not me, not me," he cried, and keeled over in a dead faint. His wife, seated outside the interview room, heard the cry and the thump when he fell off his chair and cried piteously: "Don't hit him, don't hit him. He didn't mean to do it."

They moved him into a cell and went to the telephone. In a very short time, certain Customs officers on both sides of the water would be ducking into dark cars, flanked by burly men. A racing certainty, that these men who sealed the truck and waved it through knew it carried more than tobacco. Such trusted officials require more than a cut from a minor racket to persuade them to go bent. Some are planted, of course. Whether these were remained for other policemen to find out. They went off now for coffee, very pleased about it all and with Clovis yet to do. He could wait until they brought him back from the hospital.

14

Things were certainly turning up nicely for Rosher. Even while the drugs men were busying themselves with his little scoop, and the man himself was closeted for his first neck-bristling review of the murder case with an equally bristling Chief Superintendent (Percy) Fillimore, Detective Inspector Young Alec Cruse, coordinator of all team effort and scrutinizer of the multifarious bumph gathering around that case, was receiving reports still from men in the field who were plodding doggedly on as they had been since they were assigned, oblivious to sudden-flaring side issues.

It was one among a batch coming in now that creased his handsome (so some said; he couldn't see it, himself) forehead. He wondered if Percy and Old Blubbergut, either or both, would spot this small thing, among so much bumph. Perhaps he'd better have a word, touchy old bastards though both of them were. Probably meant nothing, but you never know. The case was hanging fire, they might as well follow this up.

This closeting of Rosher with the old arch enemy had so far not advanced the cause. They simply were incompatible, that's all, molded by God for His inscrutable amusement into the perfect personality clash. Neither tried to hide the antipathy any more. Certainly not Rosher, barking curtly as they went together through reports and he clarified for the other man whatever he was asked, curtly, to clarify. And Percy was no better, putting the needle in automatically to further redden the reddened neck. As when he pushed the bumph aside and snapped disparagingly: "Don't appear to have got very far, do you?"

Unjust. And totally without foundation. Rosher might well have pointed out that so far as the murder case went, it was still very early days; and by God he'd come up with a cracker on the side, hadn't he? Instead, goaded as ever by this narrow-eyed man, he barked: "Doesn't matter now you've got it, does it? Ought to be cleared by lunchtime."

"I suggest, Mr. Rosher," snapped Percy, who knew heavy sarcasm when he heard it, "that you moderate your tone." He rearranged the paper into a neat pile. Always very neat, his desk was. "Well, I shall go down there, see what I can do for myself. You—er—need not accompany me, I prefer to form my own view of the matter. No doubt you can find plenty to occupy yourself with here, what with one thing and another."

Did you ever? What a way for responsible ranking policemen to carry on. What Percy was doing, of course, was brushing the inspector off his shoulder, and managing further disparagement while he did it. He even managed to sniff disdain onto Rosher's triumph by reducing it to one thing and another. He had a potent sniff, honed to a fine edge by many years of deep snuffing at nasal decongesteants in obedience to his hypochondria. Impressive when done with one nostril, tube inserted and finger over the other, it was doubly so when both were free and used together.

Now Inspector Rosher was more than willing to be out of Percy's company. He never asked to be in it. He saw no pleasure and no point in stumping again over the old ground. Whatever was there, he'd seen and gathered. Better to stay here, writing his report, catching up on his backlog of bumph, available should the drugs lads need him, studying and mulling over the paper accrued around the murder. He grunted: "Grrmph." No more than that. And he turned upon his heel.

So it was that when Detective Inspector Young Alec Cruse arrived with his papers to knock upon Percy's door, the man was gone out in his light overcoat and soft felt hat. Having verified by peeping in that it was so, Young Alec moved on, down from cocoanut matting underfoot to compo flooring, where he clacked along the passage and knocked on Inspector Rosher's door. Inspector Rosher barked, to declare his presence behind it.

He was sitting behind his desk, hunched like a gorilla brooding the pros and cons of God and Charles Darwin. Young Alec said, very politely—there was lingering awkwardness in his dealing with Rosher that would never pass away—"Sorry to intrude. Just spotted a—well, it's probably nothing, but I thought you might like to . . . um . . ."

What it amounted to was this: Men had been and still were showing photographs in all the clubs, pubs, discos, and places where youth might be expected to foregather, in the town and the big city and all around. Routine. Do you know this lad? It seemed by the reports that some of them did; and mostly these were clubs that would have been raided out of existence in the good old days. Now you can do it without let or hindrance, provided you are a consenting adult and so is he.

"Mm," said Rosher, when the young man finished. "Uh-huh. Mm. Okay. Right. Leave it with me."

Young Alec went away. Inspector Rosher spent a little time on the phone, ringing those clubs to see if they could tell him more about the visits of John Patrick O'Hara. Only one call was answered, and nothing came from that. Clubs that trade late into the night are normally closed in the morning. When he was done with the phone, he put it down and sat for a while gently tapping his great brownstone incisors with a pencil. Then he got up, and reached for the black hat.

He went to Mavourneen's house. She said: "Och—hello, then, Mr. Rosher. I thought you might be calling. What a morning. You've arrested the Chafers and everybody, there's hell to pay all over, and they took Brendan last night. Will you be coming in, herself is upstairs, she's been raising hell because the pub's not open." All this with excitement, and a sort of breathless coyness. The Irish, excited, let it all out in a sparkling stream. Sexual stirring shows in the eyes.

"'Morning," said Rosher. "Yes, I'll just . . ." and he stepped into the hall. Upstairs, a door slammed. The Widow O'Hara appeared, bearing down the stairs in quite the old style, crying as she came: "Phwhat d'ye tink ye're doing, den, closing down te public houses and shtarving souls wit dere tongues hanging out not able to get a dhrop?"

"Oh, shut up, Mother," Mavourneen cried, at least as loudly. And as the crone came to hall level, making for Rosher with seemingly belligerent intent, she grabbed her by the arm and bustled her down the passage and into the kitchen. Gnashing as she went, the old lady twisted her head before being vanished, to screech: "Why don't ye catch te swoine dat did it to my Johnnie, instead of going about deproiving dacent people of dere lawful Guinness?"

Mavourneen shut the door and locked it. The key was in the lock and ready, so perhaps the kitchen was used regularly to seal the old lady in. The daughter brought her bosom back to Rosher. "Sorry about that," she said. "Can I be offering you a cup of tay?" A thumping as of fists came on the kitchen door. She lifted her voice. "Shut up now, you old bat, and get yourself some cornflakes."

Bit late for cornflakes, Rosher thought. But then, some people eat them like sweeties. He said: "No, thank you." Declining the cup of tea.

"You've only just missed your other feller," she said. "Thin feller, mean look. Gray coat and a soft felt hat; he was here not five minutes ago. Superintendent, he said he was."

"Uh-huh." Percy, going the full round. Bound to call here first. Rosher had scanned for his car before he knocked. "I've called about your nephew. Was he homosexually inclined?" The bludgeon approach.

She opened her mouth as if to deny it vigorously, hotly as Catholic people must deny such imputation against a family member, brought up as they are to believe it is all pretty degraded, but homosexuality quite the worst of it, anathema to Pope and God alike. Mind you, masturbation is not to be sniffed at. Then she hesitated. And then she said:

"I—may I be forgiven for it—I have . . . wondered. There was . . . I wondered about Brendan's suddenly appearing like that and Johnnie saying it was all right they'd share his room. And there was—er. Will you hang on here for a minute?"

She turned and went upstairs, returning almost immediately with a smallish photograph, which she gave him. It showed Johnnie and three close friends. Very close, judging by the way their cheeks nestled together and their arms hung about each other. They take these pictures in gay clubs where everybody is letting his hair down. They take them in heterosexual clubs, too, but the protagonists are usually mixed. In a sense, they were here. One of the characters wore drag. "I happened to find it," Mavourneen said. "I was sorting through his things. They're the fellers in the souvenir shop, aren't they?"

"Mm," said Rosher. "I'll take this with me, if it's all right with you." He tucked the picture into his wallet and turned to leave.

The bosom moved forward, the lashes fluttered in a simper matching that worn by her nephew in the photograph. "Are you sure I can't give you a cup of tay?" she said. "Or anything you might be fancying." And loudly, as hammering came upon the kitchen door: "Will you shut up, now, before I come in to you?"

"Thank you, no," said Rosher, and he got out of there.

By the book, he should have notified Percy before proceeding to the hospital. He could have had the station pass a message on by radio. But bugger Percy, let him piss about wherever he wanted to. He, Rosher, had the first possible thin wedge here, and it could lead on to more kudos yet. When the ball comes your way, kick the bloody thing. Don't pass it to the opposition.

Clovis lay in bed in a private annex attached to the public ward with the bedclothes up to his chin. They would be moving him soon, to a cell under the station, but no one had bothered to tell him. One guard he had, and nobody had pressed him as yet. The drugs people had been in, much earlier, and gone away again. He was very whoozy then. He'd keep.

The whooziness was gone now, ebbing gradually to leave a wonderful, weird peace in which his mind floated, playing with bubblelike thoughts: of Peter—the treacherous—the beautiful—the beloved—the dead. All his thoughts were of Peter, and for this while, he felt no pain. He felt nothing but the lapping and sighing of peace. Then the gorilla walked in, black-hatted and bandy, saying to the constable left beside the bed: "All right, lad. Just want a word with his nibs here."

"Ah," said the constable. He knew Inspector Rosher well. "Yeah. All right. Only he's—er—the junk boys . . ."

"Yes yes yes." The inspector waved him aside. "Just sit and study your navel, this is the other matter."

He's not supposed to be disturbed, the constable thought, and began to frame it into words. But Rosher had fixed stern eyes on the man in bed, he was saying: "Well, my son. Landed ourself in it, haven't we?"

The abrasive tone cut into Clovis's peace. The sense of well-being that can follow pump-out of an overdose is completely spurious, and eggshell fragile. His eyes focused sharply on the gorilla's stern face as the camera lens stopped down moves from nebulous fuzziness to pitiless clarity.

He saw, alarmingly, all the seamed leatheriness of skin, the formidable blueness of jowl, the implacable little eye under the ridged brow. He saw the black hat. He saw the movement of leather lips, and heard the hostile voice bark: "You're right up the proverbial, my lad, and you haven't got a paddle, have you? Time we had a little chat, you and me."

"I don't want . . . I don't want . . ." said Clovis.

"Never mind what *you* want, lad," Inspector Rosher said. "I'll tell you what *I* want. I want cooperation. And if I don't get it, I'll have your guts instead."

Oh, charming, thought the listening constable. How do we stand after that, with Judges' Rules?

Old Blubbergut was speaking again. "You lied to me, lad, didn't you? You told me a fib, and that's naughty. You told me you only knew John O'Hara by sight."

Clovis was not thinking of Johnnie. He had been concentrating on Peter. The deflection startled him. He said: "I—I didn't."

"Oh yes you did, it's all in the book. Too late to deny it now." The inspector produced a photograph. "So how do you explain this?"

"Ha," said Clovis. "That was, that was. . . . Ha."

"Well may you say ha, my son," the gorilla said. "Know what I'm going to do? I'm going to pin his murder on you."

Really, thought the policeman, we shouldn't be carrying on like this. In the station, yes, and the privacy of a cell. But who knows in a hospital what walls bristle with ears? What if Matron is in the office next door, lug pressed to a specimen bottle, the open end against the plaster?

"He was, he wasn't . . ." said Clovis. "I didn't—we . . ."

"Better speak up, lad. I'm going to have you, be sure of it."

Clovis was in no state to consider that Rosher was pulling the well-known stroke. With no proof, nothing at all to go on, he was using pure, outrageous hammer tactics in the hope that something might be whacked out of the subject to lead—somewhere. A common police ploy. Nor was he given hint of drug charges awaiting him so grave that in terms of porridge, murder clapped on top could hardly make any difference. He'd been unconscious during all the kerfuffle, and too whoozy when the Drugs Squad called to take in what they were saying. But he understood murder. Murder is an emotive word; the thought that he might be fitted up with it is liable to induce panic, in any bent.

And he had, of course, been with Johnnie that night, the night he disappeared. He said: "I didn't know him, I met him . . . at parties. . . ."

"Like this one?" Rosher indicated the photograph. "All girls together, eh? I like the pink frock, it suits you. Doesn't *look* as though you don't know him, does it?"

"That was, we were only. . . . That was a party."

"When?"

"I—don't know."

"Do you have 'em all the time, then? Get 'em mixed up, do you?" No answer. Subject was twitching now about the nostrils. The hard man carried on. "Four little poofters. What do you play at these parties? Bugger Your Neighbor? Piggy-in-the-Middle?"

Oh, I say, I say, the policeman was thinking, leave off, do. The pouf was saying: "You have no right—"

"Don't tell *me* what I have a right to do, lad. I'll tell *you*. I've a right to stitch you up, and I'm going to do it. And it's no good looking at my friend over there, he's got a guide dog and he's stone deaf."

Clovis's eyes had indeed rolled sideways, imploringly, to where the policeman sat. And this man was thinking: Oo, bloody hell. If the old twat dropped in over this, I go with him now, don't I, if I don't jump up and deny it? And how can I do that? By the time he had thought this, Rosher had pressed on and it was too late.

"When did you see O'Hara last?"

"I—don't remember." Spoken from the pure instinct embedded in the bent: when pressed, evade everything. But even as he said it, Clovis knew it for a mistake. His eyes had seen the photo: himself, Peter, Johnnie, Brendan. And Brendan still alive. And Brendan, Johnnie's boyfriend, was with him at the party, that last night of Johnnie's life. If this terrible gorilla had not already seen him, if he was not about to leap in and nail him, Clovis, with the lie, he would certainly see him, Brendan, soon.

With the inspector's hard and beady eyes upon him, Clovis swallowed; spoke again. "Yes. I do. We had . . . a party. The Blue Boar Club." And a right den of campology that is, the listening constable thought.

Rosher barked. "When?"

"The night before—the night of the fire."

"And?"

"I, we all left together."

"Who's all?"

"Me and . . . Peter. And Johnnie and Brendan. They were—friends. Brendan and Johnnie. Johnnie was, he'd been drinking."

"And?"

"We dropped them off. Outside our place. They went . . . home."

"How do you know where they went?"

"I—I—" said Clovis, and burst suddenly into tears, screaming as a woman will. "Leave me alone! Leave me alone!"

Now you've done it, the constable thought, startled. Pressed him too hard. You won't get any more out of him, he's gone hysterical. Bloody hell, he can't half screech. Goes right through you.

Footsteps pattered in the stone corridor outside. The ward sister hurried in. "What's going on here?" she demanded. "What are you doing to that man?"

"I am a police officer, madam," the inspector barked, above the caterwauling.

She knew what he was, she had ushered him in. But she barked right back. Sisters are not easily intimidated, standing on ground that is theirs by right. "I don't care what you are, you can't come in here doing what you're doing, you can hear it right over in Gurnet Ward." She crossed to the bed, shouted at Clovis—she had to shout, to be heard above his screaming—"That's enough of that, now! That's quite enough of that! Come along, now, don't be silly." She grabbed him by the shoulders, and shook him. He screamed right on, with his head snapping back and forth.

Now that is something no policeman would dare to do, lay physical hands upon a screaming suspect. It has been done, but never in front of witnesses, unless he's banging himself and the place up. Or she is; an hysterical woman can go a bit.

The matter is immaterial. Inspector Rosher had not laid his hands on anybody and he had a witness to prove it. Even his seasoned veins had bumped a little at the sheer unexpectedness of Clovis's outburst, but he was not upset by it. He would have stayed a while, to lean on the man some more; but the man was not going to scarper, he'd be here or in a cell. Not worth staying, to get into a tear-up with the hospital. These things can bounce back on you.

No: the thing to do was get back to the station, if possible before Percy returned. Because if this pouf was to be believed, the other pouf was with the dead pouf after this pouf was.

Without a word, then, as Clovis's wailing died to heart-twisted sobbing, the inspector dug in his rubber heel, turned upon it, and departed abruptly—leaving the nurse trying to remember what happened if you gave a tranquilizing drug to a person recovering from an overdose of drugs, and the resident policeman sweating lightly, thinking: Say this for Old Blubbergut. You can tell when he's been around.

15

Perhaps not all over town, but in the immediate vicinity of Inspector Rosher it was a hard day for gays. Not a gay day at all; they kept bursting into tears.

Thus, when the man bandied into the station after a fast drive from the hospital, he snapped to Sergeant Barney Dancey, on duty in the reception area: "Percy back yet?"

"Nope," said Barney. Quite mildly. He had known Rosher a

long time, to be snapped at by him brought no umbrage. "Haven't seen him."

"Hmph," said Rosher, and went straight to the CID room, into which he poked his head. "Who's doing nothing?"

Caught by the abrupt bark and with no time to become busy, one of the four men present suspended his crossword puzzling and said: "Er..."

"Come with me, then. Bring your book." The grim, black-hatted head vanished. The young detective constable sighed, put aside his paper, and rose to his feet. "Hard luck, mate," his good buddies said as they lapsed back into torpor. Torpor comes rarely to a police station, between times of frenzied activity. When it comes, it is cherished.

Old Blubbergut was at the bottom of the steps leading to basement cells by the time the young man caught up, and the jailer constable was rattling his keys, selecting the one that unlocked a floor-to-ceiling barred gate giving into the cell corridor. Rosher must have told him already whom he was here to see, because when they were through the jailer led on without a word to unlock the cell occupied currently by Brendan Mulcahy, latest in a long line of incumbents who have been saturating it in sin and sorrow for more than a hundred years.

Brendan was sitting huddled on the narrow bunk, at the far end close to the wall. Few people walk about once their belt and braces have been taken away, because the trousers tend to fall down. And shoes are not too manipulable without laces. He wore the coarse issue blanket clutched like a shawl over his shoulders and he looked as if he were shivering. He gazed at the policemen as they came in, apprehensively from his mauve-ringed, filly-lashed Irish eyes.

It was almost too easy. Of course it was. The lad was overmatched, sitting there with the towel already fluttering in. Shattered by the accusation that he was involved in drug smuggling, his desperate spate of earlier talk had evaded all mention of Johnnie, and nobody had referred to him. But he had not really believed that nobody would. Inexperienced prisoners left alone to brood in a cell commonly build up a nightmare in which the police are omnipotent, knowing much more than they actually do. The leave-'em-alone technique is used deliberately to foster this condition. So here was Brendan, all ready to crumble when Inspector Rosher barked without charity: "I am here to question you regarding the murder of John Patrick O'Hara."

And straightway, the lad burst into tears. They sprang full-fledged from those eyes, they coursed down the greeny-white cheeks, the Celtic nose, the pointed chin, and were plashing already onto the government blanket as he cried in a curious, strangled voice: "It wasn't murder! It wasn't murder!"

The inspector was still wearing his black hat, and not a trace of pity showed in the little eyes gimlet-sharp beneath the grim brim. "Carry on," he barked. "Let's be hearing from you."

Yet another young policeman's mind leaped with quick alarm to wonder how this stood with Judges' Rules. The wonder was fleeting, the alarm equally so. This one wouldn't raise it in court, he was as ready to squawk as a hopped-up Myna bird.

"I didn't do it." He was weeping, rocking his plashing head about. "I didn't do it, I didn't do it."

"All right, my son," said Inspector Rosher. "Let's have it from where you left the party." And to the constable: "Get a chair in from outside. And stand by your notebook."

Mention of the party completed, if completion were necessary, the jellification of Brendan. They knew about the party. Ergo, as he had known they did, they knew about everything. More than ever was he eager to talk, in obedience to a fundamental Irish trait that believes garrulity will somehow soften retribution.

Within five minutes, he was confessed. He told how he and Johnnie were left outside the flat shared by Peter and Clovis. Johnnie had been drinking. They all had; but Johnnie with drink taken became erratic. Boisterous. At times, obstreperous.

That night his mood had veered between bellicose and lachrymose. Both conditions erupted around interest shown in Brendan by a middle-aged and very butch-looking gentleman at the party, who winked and smirked from one of the Blue Boar tables. Johnnie, catching him at it, glanced swiftly at Brendan and caught the answering smile and a flick of the long lashes. That did it.

Johnnie was away, to sort the man out. It passed over without bloodshed. The man was charming, conciliatory, poured them champagne—even gave Johnnie a couple of cigars. No punch-up, the party went on. Middle-aged queers are not without experience in handling these situations. But the incident, plus perhaps the champagne on top of party intake, had told on Johnnie's mood.

The fact of having to walk home after they left Clovis and Peter bothered Brendan. It was not far—a couple of hundred yards brought them to the bridge, and beyond it to the cul-de-sac street between abandoned warehouses where Sydney's truck would rest the following night. Along here, through the gate and across the transport yard to the alley that came out close to Mavourneen's house, and there you were. Easy enough, with your wits in order you need not be seen at all. But a well-pickled Irishman hurling loud accusation, even weeping, can attract attention in post-midnight streets. Respectable people may be in bed, but the police will not. And with tobacco on his mind, Brendan was at all times chary of the police.

Sure enough, Johnnie had bristled the walk with nervous tension. He called Brendan many kinds of whore, and then he wept and implored forgiveness for doing so. It was only because he loved him, he said. A very fraught ten minutes; but nobody about. Until they were right at the top end of the alley, and emerging into Mavourneen's street. A hundred yards to go, no more. And there was the beat man, a night-patrolling policeman, walking leisurely this way between them and the house.

The police, the dreaded police. No chance of passing unseen. No chance of passing unquestioned, two late-bird Irishmen both with drink taken, one drunk and voluble with a tear-stained face and smoking a cigar. Because Johnnie had paused in the alley to light up the gift not smoked at the party; and Brendan had decided not to demur, so close to home, for fear of starting him off again. Almost there. Get home quick, that was the thing.

Now, they couldn't. The policemen would certainly have seen

them—Johnnie's cigar end glowing and all—had he not at this moment lowered his head, shining his lamp on his watch to check the time. Mind you, they were open to scrutiny only for a flash before Brendan had Johnnie back in the alley and on the way to the other end, not knowing if they had been seen or not. And Johnnie came now without argument. He, too, had the guilty Irishman's sensitivity to sudden alarm; because when Brendan told the police he alone distributed the tobacco, it was as part of his general fending off to questions relating to Johnnie, who in fact got rid of a lot of it, and had since only he and Sydney were concerned in the caper. Something cut through his drunken state when Brendan bundled him back into that alley. He took off willingly. Say run to the little bent, and drunk or sober up go the knees.

Brendan checked the retreat at the haulage yard and peered back, all but his eyes and a sliver of head tucked away round the corner. And he saw the policeman enter the alley, only because at that end a street lamp cast a little light. They'd been seen. "Come on," he whispered, and urged Johnnie onward.

That policeman entered that alley only to be rid of his last cup of canteen tea. Knowing this, given their turn of mind they might have lingered, to view formidable matters of great interest. If, that is, they could have seen by that dim light. As it was, they took off before the zip was down, headed for the one place both knew where they could be under cover and out of sight.

The warehouse, of course. Where the tobacco was stored—and the drugs, although neither of them knew this. Entered, not from this, the yard side, but from the fire-break wynd between this and the next-door warehouse, where Clovis and Peter had their shop.

To any but the initiate, the building was boarded up, ground-floor windows and doors. But the select few knew that at a window in the wynd you slipped a hand through the boards, which had been cunningly attached to a frame, and felt for a latch. Slip it up, push so the boards swung inward, and in you went. Close the gap behind you and tread very carefully, avoiding the rotten boarding by stepping on the beams. Simple enough; their course was quite obvious—in daylight, or armed with a lamp. These two had no lamp. No light in the pitch blackness but the faint glow from Johnnie's cigar.

All this comes to you very much more smoothly and in far greater detail than it went to Rosher. He received an outline only, forced out through tears, prodded out with questions, at time almost babblingly incoherent. It didn't matter. Any long-steeped copper can fill in the details in capers of this kind, and what he leaves for now he will rake in later. Sitting on a wooden chair brought in by his acolyte, he let the huddled, shivering lad weep it out, snapping when the narrative needed pushing on. Like now, as Brendan faltered to a halt.

"Carry on, lad. Carry on."

"He . . . fell through," said Brendan. "He was . . . drunk . . . he missed the beams, the floor—was rotten. He was stuck. I tried to pull him back. . . ." Only his head and shoulders jutting, and his arms. "I couldn't see. It was dark. . . ." Pitch dark. "And then there were—flames—underneath, in the basement." Littered with old wool, bale wrappings, the whole place steeped in grease, all highly combustible. "He must have . . . dropped his . . . cigar. . . ."

"And?"

"He—fell right through. The flames were . . . I couldn't hold him." He didn't even scream. A thump—and nothing. Only the swift-growing flames, lurid now, licking at the hole left when he vanished. It was a concrete floor down there; if you hit your head falling onto it you wouldn't scream, even though you fell into fire. One inward breath would do for you.

The lad came to a complete halt again, shuddering with his hands pressed over his eyes. Rosher's voice spoke almost gently, softened not by pity but because a skilled operator does not push two questionees in quick succession into a state of incoherent hysteria. It wastes time, and is frowned upon.

"What did you do? Leave him there?"

"I . . . couldn't get down there. It—I—ran out. To the—there's a phone . . . by the bridge . . . I rang 999 . . . but it was vandalized. . . ."

And then he ran on. Blindly, panicked, seeking in terror a phone booth in working order; seeing above rooftops the lurid glow rising; fleeing at last for home, entering over the outhouse roof and through the window into the one hole in which he could huddle, alone and stricken with the horror of it, seeing the glare, hearing the up-risen people talking, the banshee howl of fire engines. Trying then to blot it all out, Mavourneen's pillows over his head.

It was the truth, the whole truth. Rosher recognized it. A man whose whole life has been given to sifting truth from lie knows which one he has been listening to. He rose from the little wooden chair, saying: "All right, lad. I'll be back for the details later, we'll need a signed statement."

No point in saying more. Brendan was not hearing him. Time to get up to the Top Brass, nail this as his before Percy got back. He nodded to his witness acolyte to put away his notebook and bring the chair, and they moved out. The cell door clanged upon another poor sinner, weeping his broken heart away.

There was nothing broken about Rosher's heart. On the contrary, it was leaping around on a singing sea of elation. The entire barrel chest and all the solid structure of head and belly and hairy, stalwart limbs seethed with it. He'd done it—he'd grabbed the bloody lot.

Who could take it from him: the drugs caper, and now this? Nobody. Certainly not Percy—he never even got his nose in. With difficulty Rosher restrained the urge to break into a veritable knees-up, clacking back with the young detective constable along the cell corridor.

When they got to the top of the stone stairs Percy was there, just coming in abundant haste through the street door. This haste was founded upon what he saw as good and sufficient reason. Nothing gained from his visiting and prodding over the canal area. When he got into his car to return, he made a radio check call to the station, to say he was coming and to gather whatever was to be known.

He learned that Inspector Rosher had visited the hospital where Clovis lay—saying not a word to him, Percy—and immediately after, as soon as he was in through the station door, had gone down to the cells. He was down there now.

This was enough for Percy. Anger flared in him at once. The man was at it again, spitting upon the deference due to rank, spurning the very book, going his own way regardless. And the bastard had a way of snatching things out of the air, under the very nose. By luck. Pure luck. Without it, he'd have been flung out of the force years ago. And rightly.

And the luck could be holding. He might—his actions suggested it—be onto something. Something that, revealed to Percy, would have been Percy's. Down went the narrow but heavy foot, and he entered the station in haste just as Inspector Rosher came up the stairs and into the reception hall. Mr. Fillimore snapped: "Ah, Mr. Rosher. May I ask what you are doing?"

No superintendent should speak in that tone and fling such a question at any detective inspector. Dammit, an inspector is not the office boy. The young detective constable melted himself away. Get out of the line of fire, if there was going to be a shoot-out. Everybody knew about these two. And look at Percy's face.

Rosher's face, too, had taken on its hard, implacable look; but it was surface, pure surface. For once—surely the first, the only time?—he met Percy with his heart singing. He said, brusquely because that was the way he addressed the man: "Nothing." Out came his big handkerchief.

Did he say it deliberately to provoke? How can a man coming like a serge-clad great ape up from cells where arrestees are packed practically eyeball to eyeball be doing nothing?

If Percy had wattles, they flushed crimson as he snapped the line that gave Rosher the game, the set, the match, and the moment that glowed in memory ever after. In Barney Dancey's memory, too, because he was there behind the desk. He snapped: "Nothing? Nothing? I take it you are aware that we are engaged on a murder inquiry?"

Rosher accepted it gratefully, the glorious topping-up of a cup already running over. The grim face remained impassive; but a glint shot about in his eye as he said: "Oh, that. You don't have to worry about that, I just cleared it.'' And he raised that great gray handkerchief, to send a triumph of trumpets blaring through the solid marble halls.

Some days went scudding by, with feasting and carousing in the soul of Inspector Rosher. He appeared again on television; he spoke with cut-glass joviality upon the local radio; the city, town, and county press bannered the caper in headlines and ran a front-page picture in which his little eyes could be seen distinctly beaming from the brim-shadow of the black hat, and the grim lips curved upward and outward to display the formidable teeth. There were commendations about, a veritable cornucopia of kudos. And best thing of all: Detective Chief Superintendent (Percy) Fillimore, bypassed and almost entirely ignored, walked about as one being rapidly devoured by spleen and terminal swine fever.

But feasting palls at last, and reaction sets in. When his rest day arrived, the inspector stayed in his cluttered and dusty house on the hill and succumbed to the sag of spiritual indigestion. Had someone been there to do it to, he would have snapped their head off, all day long. So Mavourneen picked quite the wrong time to visit.

She came because—well—why does a woman set out to see a man when he has vanished for a week, during which he has been lauded on her very telly screen; she being lonely and under stress and in dire need of a bull-bollocked masculine strength such as she has known in him since childhood? And the grapevine saying his wife was gone, that he was living in lonely squalor up there in that house.

She climbed up to him on foot. Having no car she traveled by bus, and it dumped her, of course, in the valley. She carried unaided the great weight of those enormous knockers—nay, say wangers, rather—right up that hill. It speaks volumes.

Inspector Rosher was frying lunch when the doorbell rang. Two beefburgers sizzled in the pan and he was cutting slabs of bread to trap them in. He put aside the knife, turned down the gas—so often as a young copper he had been called to chip-pan fires—and padded his slippers through his dust-motey hall. She stood upon the doorstep and smirked upon him, panting lightly. "Ah," he said.

The smirk grew wider. She had on her good suit and the hat she wore for weddings. "Hello, there," she cried gaily, with a wag of the fingers that conjured up fleetingly the late, great Oliver Norvil Hardy. "I rang the station, they said you was on your rest day. Just thought I'd pay you a visit."

The second she batted her lashes, he thought: Sod you. He said, brusquely: "What for?"

"Just—well—just to see how you are getting on." The teeth gleamed, the brogue came rich as Doubledums Fruit Cake (the Fruitier Fruit Cake).

"Grrrmph," he said.

"Will you not be asking a body in now, for a cup of tay?" she said. "It's spitting dry I am after the hill." They were right—she could see the neglected hall behind him. In squalor, himself was living. Needed a woman, if only to look after him.

But Rosher was thinking: Oh no. He knew well enough what it means when a bolster-busted lady arrives simpering on the doorstep, panting lightly. Let this one in, you'd never get her out. He said, in the authentic Blubbergut bark: "I should stay away from me, madam, if I were you. I'm a policeman."

That bark hit her in the simper; but she was a game girl, with her heart set one way. She pursued it and said: "More than a policeman. Much more than a policeman. . . ."

"A policeman," he barked. "And I would advise you that you may be coming under investigation"

Now the simper slipped. "What—what for?" she said.

"Allowing your house to be used for the storing of illegal merchandise."

One hand came up to the bolster. "I never did!" she said.

Probably she didn't. Not knowingly. But it was a fair bet that with the nephew and Mulcahy both distributing, they rested it there. Wouldn't be going all the time into that warehouse.

"We have reason to believe that you did," he barked. "Also that you harbored known criminals. And there's the matter of subletting council property. I should stay well away from me, madam, if I were you.''

All rubbish, of course, Nobody, least of all him, would bother to probe the possibility that she knew smuggled tobacco was in the house. And the lads were not known criminals at all. As for subletting council property—tush. Flim-flam. But Rosher knew what he was doing.

She was white now, the simper blasted completely away; mouth slightly open, eyes suddenly shocked and apprehensive. ''I swear to God,'' she said, ''I haven't done a ting.''

Firmly, he closed the door.